A Royally Fake French Menage

A Rippton Creatives Fake Dating Castle Romance

Sofia Aves

First Edition

Cover by JayJay Book Designs

EBOOK ISBN 978-1-923471-08-5.

PRINT ISBN 978-1-923471-09-2

The ex, the crush, and the castle.

That's what my weekend in France should have been called. I didn't mean to invite her, and I sure as hell didn't mean to run into *him*. But that happened, and so did a few other things.

The question... is how do I leave France without wrecking three hearts? Because my family thinks my fake date with her is real, and they'll never approve of my relationship with him.

But then, I've always been a bit... Different.

And neither of them seem to mind.

CONTENT INSTRUCTIONS

There are no warnings for this book. The blurb and cover told you exactly what it was about. If you've changed your mind, that's okay. The exit is over there by the coffee stand. Barclay understands, and he'll never take offense. He might flirt with you on the way out, so just keep an eye on him. He doesn't move fast but he really can sashay, though he does trip on his bow tie occasionally.

Check the shadows for Jacques. He'll never announce himself. And Genie will name her next line after the color of... Something.

Now that's done, be prepared. Barclay thinks he knows how to play but it's been a long time since he's been in France, and longer still since he saw an old...

friend. And he never, not once, brought home a crush while he was there.

At least, not one he really cared about, or a female.

So I guess it is a warning, after all. Because one of them is a flirt.

One is curious.

And one is so possessive that they'll do anything for the person they've loved for a long, long time.

Actually, no. Wait. Sorry. I spelled obsession wrong.

And that can be catastrophic.

Sofia xx

On the days your skin doesn't fit,
Wear it as it sits.

CHAPTER ONE

BARCLAY

"**D**o *you want to come on a date to a castle? Not a real one, just a fake one."*

Those were the words that fell out of my mouth as I stared down at the prettiest little thing Rippton U had to offer.

Genie Lockwood.

My long term crush of four months and three days. The longest I'd ever had in this country. She was cute, sweet, and nothing like my fucked up mess of an ex on campus

And I screwed my chances with her the moment I ballsed up enough to ask her out. At least, I thought I did.

But as always, Genie surprised me.

"The castle, or the date?" She tilted her heart shaped face up and pierced me with those burnt honey eyes that read the lies etched on my soul.

Genie stood in the middle of the campus commons on a perfectly bright, cheery morning, and fuck me did sunshine lance through my soul when she stared at me like that.

"I do beg your pardon?" Twenty-one years of immaculate chevalier training on both my English and French lineage sides kicked in to preserve my pasty ass with an excess of manners.

"Barclay Augustus Chesterfield. Pay attention." She snapped nude and pale pink tipped nails in my face. Something in her hazel gaze softened the gesture, along with a little booty shake that I could have drooled over for the rest of the afternoon. Or at least until the sun set across campus. "Which one is the fake part? I mean, a crappy cardboard castle sounds terrible but a fake date, I can do." She smiled brightly, though her hazel eyes remained curious.

Now she thinks I'm a fucking loon. Not that she'd be wrong.

I coughed into my fist, my cheeks heating as a pretty girl watched me with equally pretty eyes. "Uh, no. The castle is real." *Two actually. Depending*

on the country in question. *Shit, is my English pass-*
port out of date this year?

The things I couldn't do for myself without paid
help about. All the product of a misspent you, if I'd
had one at all.

"Awesome." Genie bounced a little on the balls
of her feet and beamed at me. Damn if the sun didn't
glow a little brighter, and angels didn't fall from the
heavens to worship at her delicate toes. "Where are
we going?"

"France?" I winced as her eyebrows rose a fraction. "I mean, that's where the family dinner is, and I
need a date. It's about two hours out of Paris. And... I
might have told my mother I had a plus one," I
muttered, breaking eye contact and tried not to
wince as I studied my tan loafers.

Fail.

Not my finest moment. I'd admit it, if only to
myself.

"Okay." She smiled up at me when I risked a
glance, all cute and stunning and so fucking
droolworthy.

I closed my mouth with a wet-sounding snap and
managed not to get my excess of saliva on her fluffy
fuchsia cardigan. "You're coming?" I couldn't keep
the surprise out of my tone.

"I mean, I'll be your fake date, Barclay." She shimmied her shoulders, that same cheeky glint in her eye.

Wait. Was my crush *flirting* with me? I gawked at her long enough that I nearly missed her next words. "What?"

"When is it?"

Genie still wore that curiosity-over-conflict expression, but rather than being shy like I expected, she looked more... Excited.

I nodded like a fucking bobble head dog that needed a short leash *now*. Maybe she could hold it for me. "You know, I've had a crush on you for the last two years." *Way to spill the beans, Barclay.*

Maybe I should just move back to France and stay there. Or England, though the staff would probably eat me alive. Coming to the USA had seemed like a fun idea. An escape. A game to play. An easy merge away from an overbearing stepmother once my father's funeral was over and I had no reason to stay any longer.

And all it did was make me complacent.

I needed more than a fake date and a weekend in a castle that had never been home to recall the mantle of the title I hated.

Barclay Augustus Chesterfield, Marquess of La Borde, France, and Marquess of Bracksley, England.

Dual titles. Though of course neither talked about the other.

And so America has seemed a simple solution. Leave it all behind and...play.

Two years I'd been at Rippton U where I enrolled my English French noble ass to get the fuck out of Dodge... Or at least shy as far away from my responsibilities as an ocean or two would allow, depending on my departure route.

The elite private college in California seemed a good place to make new friends, discover fresh enemies and screw everything that walked past without regard to gender. Being away from France provided the ulti-mate freedom for which I paid a hefty price tag, though the multimillion dollar personal tithe all students on campus paid barely scratched the surface of my bank happy nine figure conglomerate account.

And now, it was time to go back. Last night I'd received a summons from my stepmother which sent me into a spiral I hadn't been able to dig myself out of until one excellent roommate in Nick Jessop offered a solution:

Homemade moonshine, the promise of an epic

hangover and a liquid based brainstorming session. I was always up for a new challenge.

And, as it turned out, I did receive my pickled inspiration, if only to blurt my idea out to the crush I'd had for nearly my entire tenure on campus.

Genie laughed, a tinkling sound that turned every head in the courtyard. "Of course, I know you've been crushing on me, Barclay." She patted my arm tracing her nails across my sleeve. Gooseflesh rippled beneath where she couldn't see, thankfully. "The trip will be fun. When do we leave?"

"Tonight?" I raised both eyebrows.

Asking about mundane things like clothes, packing, or passports never crossed my mind. Genie Lockwood was heiress to one of Europe's largest luxury brands. She probably traveled more often than I did.

And just like me she was off boarded to Rippton U to learn a little American, uh, subculture. Her other mission was likely to make the connections with the other offspring of the ridiculously wealthy that would take her future empire higher.

And probably connect well enough to secure a decent marriage.

The thought left a bitter note in my mouth that

had nothing to do with Nick's ferocious blend from last night.

She smiled and tossed her hair over her shoulder. "I think I can do that. France is quite lovely. See you when you pick me up."

When I expected her to turn away, Genie caught me in her piercing gaze again, raised up onto her toes like a perfect ballet dancer, and brushed those plush, dusky pink lips across my cheek. A series of tingles sparked across my shoulders, right to the base of my spine.

"Will do," I managed to force out past dry lips, staring more like an American than the hybrid French British marquis I'd been born as, according to my paper worked pedigree.

Genie sashayed away. My eyes fell to those luxurious hips with curves just large enough to fill my palms. I wanted to hold onto her and bang all night long like my life depended on it.

A few steps along her genteel retreat, she gave a little wiggle.

I stared.

Was that a happy dance?

I shook my head and headed back to the Kingsman frat house at the far side of campus, wondering why it was suddenly me who wasn't sure what the hell I got myself into, and not her.

"Not the armor again. Jesus wept, Barclay." Beau Bennett folded his arms and blocked my progress along the upstairs hallway of the Kingsman frat house.

The house where I'd lived for the past two years and left when an offer to get the hell out of the sights of this asshole came up. Beau Bennett, Allstar jock and mafia heir, was scarier than my grandmother had ever been on my English side, and that was saying something.

I straightened, tugging on the bowtie at my throat with one finger. The urge didn't secure me enough room to breathe, though I swiped sweat from the inside of the band. I strangled the thick rope connected to the ancient chest scraping its way along the plush carpeting in my wake with the other.

Time to fess up.

"Okay, so my lazy ass didn't move all the armor last time when I left, and I need to reclaim this. Plus, I'll get castrated by someone so much worse than you if I don't take it back." *Lie.* The armor belonged to the English side but he didn't need to know the step-monster didn't need it back. I shimmied up a smile just for him. On anyone else I knew that move came across as cute, unobtrusive and maybe even a come on.

With this man? I was a nuisance to be squashed into the woolen threads of his carpet that I mangled beneath the ancient chest that bore plenty of scars.

But the concept of not returning to France without the entire contingent of family armor didn't bear thinking about. I couldn't leave anything unattended with this man lurking about, and certainly not beneath his roof a moment longer.

Beau's eyes narrowed as I became the sole focus of his attention. "Why?"

One word, and the man gave me whiplash.

I froze like a Rippton U goalie against an oncoming Blackstone U opposing team hellbent on our mutual destruction. The last time I flirted with him, Beau ended up with both the girls I wanted, fucking them each publicly on party night in full view of the frat house and then some. The whole debacle left me whimpering after my conniving ex. Becoming involved with her again turned out to be a poor choice in a long line of equally shitty decisions that night.

I moved out of the Kingsman house to get the fuck away from Bennett and his ilk the following week, preferring the mixed odd company of the rock-star, the geek, the goth girl, and the tennis champion who made up my current independent household and out of Allstar-fratboy land.

Along with the rest of the family armor.

Not taking the whole lot with me at the time seemed remiss at this point, but I hated sweat. Just another fucking poor decision on my part.

Which brought me back to the asshat blocking my path with broad shoulders and suck-me-off worthy lips.

"Move," I said tightly, flapping a manicured hand at him.

"If I don't?" Beau's dark eyes glinted as he stared me down.

I'll find the Claymore and cut off your goddam balls.

My mouth kept mum on that one, thank fucking God. Otherwise, it would've been somebody else who got castrated. My stepmother wouldn't be pleased to miss out on doing it for him.

"Move." I shoved aside my exhaustion, readying myself for the oncoming fight that I couldn't see a way around.

The Kingsman attic at the end of the hall was dry, dusty and made up of fifteen feet and twelve steps of utter hell that no one but me ventured into for the past fifty years. Sweat trickled into the crevices in my elbows, itchy fingers trailing in a slow procession to the small of my back.

I straightened to my full height and planted my feet squarely, managing to stare the jock before me down, and gained half an inch on his height thanks to the stout heels on my Italian loafers.

Beau blinked. The corner of his mouth lifted in a fleeting smile. "That was... Cute."

My dick started to harden.

"Don't fucking flirt with me," I snapped, as flustered as fuck. "Go play with some other goddamn lord, like Nelson. Doesn't he still live here? Besides, don't you have your own Toy to play with?" I trotted on out his pet term for the girl he loved to fuck not so quietly around the house with the sort of showmanship that made him forget why he clung to her so tightly int he first place.

Beau Bennet wasn't half as untouchable as he thought.

A single snarky remark, and all the humor left his face. "That wasn't smart."

I smirked, just to shit him off further. "Probably not."

"*Barclay*," cried a soft voice I recognized from the way the asshole made her scream his name and no one else's loud enough to ruin a good night's sleep for the entire household.

Those cries on nights while I lay beside my ex-girlfriend-turned-psycho left her voice utterly recognizable and me very damn lonely with my spent cock in my hand.

A dark head whipped out from behind Beau and a figure darted toward me. Slender arms engulfed me at waist chest level. The tiny woman hugged me with all the considerable strength she hid in a fun-sized package.

I rested one hand on her head, twirling the dark strands between my fingers. "How are you doing, chipmunk?"

Sylvie batted her lashes as she looked up at me, giggling. "I'm good." She snuggled for a moment longer then detached herself, glancing over her shoulder at Beau who glowered at both of us.

"If you're done." A muscle along his jaw flexed, green eyes blazing as he stared at her and then lifted his gaze to me.

Now that's some possessive alpha level shit.

I knew a man like that once. He'd been good fun to play with, for a few seasons back in France. The year when I found I had a heart, despite my mother's efforts to the contrary.

I bent down to Sylvie's level. Just to shit Beau further up the wall I kept her chin in my hand and tipped her head back so she looked straight at me as I lowered my face to hers, like I might kiss her. "Be a good little Toy, and ask your boy to move for me, honey?"

A secondary use of all his little keywords that he didn't keep mum about around the house seemed warranted.

I might be poppish, petty even. Hell, I was born that way. But if Beau Bennett thought he had the market cornered on keeping house secrets, he had a long way to go. I was raised on intrigue in English courts, and learned the names of a certain European prince's seven secret mistresses. The eighth, and most recently discarded one, taught me how to make a woman orgasm in just as many ways the hour after she left the palace.

"Say bye-bye, Toy," Beau murmured, his voice lowering the easy words into a threat.

Sylvie rolled her eyes at him and winked at me. "Move, Beau." She stepped into him, resting her hands on his abdomen. Her fingers slid down to drift across the top of his leather belt as she peered up at him through her lashes. "Don't we have other things to do?"

Beau swallowed. His larger hands cupped the back of her head, drawing her up onto her toes so he didn't have to bend down to kiss her. "Don't test me, Toy."

He only had eyes for her. A pit of absolute nothingness opened inside me for all sorts of the wrong reasons.

Taking the opportunity Sylvie granted me with her brand of distraction, I dragged my chest to armor around the soon to be snogging couple and down the hall. The strain killed my shoulders but I didn't stop, not until I made it to the top of the stairs. Only then did I glance back in time to see Beau back Sylvie into his room and had the pleasure of experiencing a second hand moan not meant for me before he kicked the door shut with a bang that reverberated across the top of the Kingsman frat house.

My exodus outside was accompanied by the sort of music I wanted to play myself, rather than witness. My mind drifted to Genie and what might—if we were lucky—awaited us in France in my ancestral home.

Or what might not.

CHAPTER TWO

GENIE

"When are you coming back to Europe to see me? You haven't picked your shade for this season's run. You need to send your feedback for my newest line. Oh, and I need your signature on the *Genie in a Bottle* range. It'll be in gold and silver across the front, so make it pretty. I'm sure Lydia sent you the paperwork."

I pretended to smile at my phone even though my mother hadn't requested a video call. "I'm sure she did. It's not like you'd handle something as basic as paperwork yourself, is it?"

My roommates rolled their eyes.

"Distraction required?" Molly mouthed at me.

I shook my head. "Got it," I mouthed back.

I'd been putting off the monthly mother call for well, a month. And she was right. I had been delaying choosing colors for the new line for way too long. But also, I'd had a lot of other distractions over the past weeks. College took on a life of its own. Exams, assignments and life in general.

"I'll pick a shade," I promised. "Send me the email again, and you'll have the signature," *From the email that was likely never sent in the first place.*

Lydia wasn't half as efficient as my mother thought her golden girl of a PA was. The personal assistant badge of honor to the world's most amazing luxury brand female CEO sat all too well on the executive's shoulders. At least, that's how Lydia saw herself as she swanned around most of her day, shopping and having lunches on my mother's time. And having seen my mother flounder financially more than once in the past, I wasn't sure how any of that added up. Thankfully, I had my own accounts unattached to hers, and my side of the business was secure.

If a little behind this year.

I flicked through my emails quickly as I chatted. Nope, no email as predicted.

Just how often Lydia *worked* for my mother was up for debate. But seeing as I hadn't exactly been pulling my end of the load, I wasn't in the ball park to whine. Then again, my mother didn't pay me a high six figure salary, either. My personal income came from my own investments or any joint projects we worked on together.

She did, however, expect me to perform on demand.

"And I'll be traveling this weekend. For a...date."

Barclay wasn't the only one who could play the fake relationship game. Pity it wasn't a real one. The European lordling would be a fun toyboy, if only for the weekend.

"Oh, Genie. Can you stretch your trip out to London? That's where the gala is this Sunday night."

My lips pulled back from my teeth in mock horror. "Who set that date? It's not even a brunch." I grew up in this world, and no one. *No. One.* Set gala dates for a Sunday night. "Wait, let me guess. It was Barnacle Bob, wasn't it? That man can sniff out charity money like tomorrow isn't actually coming."

"Tomorrow might not come for him, dear. He's

ninety-three next month. I'm sure we'll all be back for another turn about the sun with his apparently immortal behind. Be a love and pick something devastating to bring in his new season with. We need to charm the socks off him."

I frowned at the phone, suddenly wishing I'd made it a video call after all. "Why?"

Mom hesitated, and my vision tunneled in. Because my mother *never* hesitated. Ever. I could count the amount of times that woman paused for breath in my life on one hand, and once was giving birth to me. The other three times were when she was caught out cheating on various husbands, and not in the order she married them.

"Why?" I asked coyly, twirling the blue dress with red trim that Molly passed between my fingers. I shook my head. "Too patriotic," I whispered, wrinkling my nose.

"What?" snapped Mom.

"Nothing. Just picking out my dress for the weekend." I waved at the black one with sequins. LBD. An oldie but so trustworthy.

On a lark I grabbed one with silver leaf shot through the bust. Molly gave me a double thumbs up.

Desiree, my other room mate who lay on her stomach on my bed, grinned. "Perfection."

"At least you have a fan club going." I could practically hear Mom's eye roll from two oceans away, assuming she was where I thought she had situated herself today.

"They're called friends." I tried not to bristle, but then our relationship had never been as simple as mother and daughter.

Or business partners.

"As long as you look the part. Remember, if it's a chateau date, take as many dresses as you'll need for the afternoon and evening sets. They have very specific expectations, even if their royalty doesn't mean a damn thing these days," Mom murmured. "I guess I'll see you on Sunday then. London time," she reminded me. "And wow me with that shade. None of that midnight-and-fuchsia rubbish from last season. I haven't had anything perform so poorly." Mom sniffed.

"At least not since you tried to reinvent the splice. Lime and black never looked so terrible together," I answered, but I was talking to an empty line and a dead phone.

Molly cheered my comeback.

It didn't hit me until my packed bags—fuchsia

and midnight blue to suit the line that were still my favorite colors of the year regardless of my mother's preferences—stood in front of my dorm, and I waited for Barclay's driver two minutes early, where I made a mistake. Or rather, my mother had.

Because I never mentioned a fake chateau date.

But she did.

CHAPTER THREE

BARCLAY

Perched beside me in the back of the black Bugatti headed away from Paris, Genie curled on the leather like a pampered house pet. Her eyes were closed, and her breaths came slow. Which left me in the company of my mother's silent driver to transport us the two hour drive from the private airstrip outside the capital where we headed to our destination of the La Borde family estate.

Genie became my study. Not that I hadn't had my eye on her for a while now back on campus, wondering which frat party to go to that ensured we'd attend together, or how best to encourage her to drop her flirty facade that she used to keep everyone at bay. Everything she did was designed. A carefully crafted outlook that made her seem oh so likable, sociable and perfect while she flirted and fluttered without ever actually stopping to engage and *flirt*.

Apparently, all it took was asking her out on a fake date. I should have tried that one earlier. A sort of bubbly, fizzing warmth surrounded her as she dosed. Even sitting still, she buzzed with the sort of happy energy I envied on this trip.

As though she sensed me watching her, Genie's fingers fluttered at the hem of her powder blue skirt that perfectly matched the twin set my mother would wholly approve of for a European born girl educated in America.

Another mask from her personal collection. I looked forward to breaking down her perfectly manicured walls.

"Penny," she murmured, stifling the cutest kitten yawn behind her French tipped fingers.

Her wrist turned as she stretched. I caught a glimpse of out of place stripes on the inside of her pale skin before she shifted again. The brief, intimate glimpse of who she was beyond her facade flitted away.

An ache started in the hollow of my gut at the

damage. *Perhaps we're not all as perfect as we pretend after all.* I added to my collection of mental notes, knowing I would need that for later this weekend.

"I didn't want to wake you," I said quietly. My fingers itched to tuck her hair behind her ear, touch her soft skin, but we weren't there. *Yet.*

Her lips curved up a fraction, a fraction less glossy than they had been when we took off earlier. "That's...considerate."

"You seemed tired."

She slept for most of the trip, sinking into her leather seat, and declining my favorite cocktails to my disappointment. Still, she did appear to need the rest. I wasn't about to be a Beau Bennett asshole level who declared she needed to entertain me just because I was sore over losing her company for a brief period. The onslaught of my family would be enough to wear us both out over the next few days.

Besides, I liked to watch her sleeping. In a non-stalker way. The way her face softened, more than usual, left her with the sort of peace that I craved for myself. Stripping that away from her seemed unnecessarily cruel.

Genie sank into the cream leather, her head

tilted to watch me. "I think you should tell me about this weekend. What's expected of us both?"

I smirked at her, rubbing my hand over my mouth as I drank her in for the first time with her watching me since the trip began. "Most likely I should warn you about my mother." I sighed. "Genie, don't worry. You are– You'll be perfect. Don't stress on it." The terms still sounded foreign in my mouth. I reached absently for her hand, then stilled as my brain caught up with the all too easy motion.

Genie caught my fingers, curling long, curved legs beneath her as she turned to face me. Her fingertips were cool against my palm as she started a little discovery tour of the tiny scars across my knuckles, cataloguing each before moving onto the next. "I thought your hands would be smoother," she murmured. "Tell me about your family?"

Who you are?

I heard the words even if she didn't say them outright. Relaxing my muscles that wanted to clench at the concept of exposing the person I'd kept hidden for so long that I'd almost forgotten who I was for myself, I watched her fingertips skate across the back of my hand with hooded eyes.

"My stepmother's a bitch, usually in heat if there's a male present more than five years younger than her. Her ultimate weakness. My father passed a year after my birth mother, but remarried shortly beforehand. The bitch in the house isn't of my blood but she'll draw you in any way she can." My lip curled in distaste, bitter seeds blossoming across the back of my tongue.

Glazed pears and red wine sauce. That's what we'd been eating when my stepmother showcased her latest fling that left my English father in heartbreak at the dinner table in front of over sixty guests the night before he suffered massive heart failure. The moment that freshly turned earth touched his coffin was the moment I walked away from France and headed to the US.

I haven't returned since.

"She sounds like a solid replacement." Genie lifted hazel eyes that reflected the horrors of her own forced life to meet mine. "I'm sorry, Barclay."

Perhaps we are more alike than you know.

The luxury brand heiress and the displaced nobility that had no place in the world, at least on the Continent.

"Because there's a bitch who sits there in place of my own mother?" My tone ran bitter, and I didn't bother to force my mood into something happier.

Perhaps Genie was the wrong person to invite to this weekend after all.

My father should never have abandoned his English seat to chase his French obsessions. Mind, looking at Genie, I understood, at least partially. Her features were fine boned, symmetrical and stunning, at a surface level at least. I hoped I required more than a pretty face in my own relationships longer term, and didn't repeat his mistakes. But my father's run of European wives and dalliances had never made him happy since losing my mother.

"I'm sorry because both your mother and father are gone. I have...one. It's hard." Genie shifted closer to me, gliding her fingers along my forearm while her other hand traced patterns on my knee.

My heart beat a similar pattern, skipping some beats and picking up others. She leaned in closer, the heat of her brushing my chest, and my breath stalled. *I'm out of practice in this. France will eat me alive.*

My mother's household will devour me.

That she insisted I call her *mother* sickened me.

I distracted myself by memorizing all the pretty colors in Genie's hair, how her neck sloped into the collar of her knitted top as she toyed with the inner seam of my slacks at my knee. "What are you doing?"

"Making you more comfortable. You're as stiff

now as you are for some of those lectures we have at Rippton U."

Stiff isn't usually what they call me there. At least, not in the Kingsman world. Beau Bennett's world that I escaped with my chest of familial armor.

"You've been watching me?" We shared a variety of law and economics classes. I often sat a row behind to watch her out of the corner of my eye. Apparently, I wasn't the only perv in the car.

Genie leaned forward and settled her chest against my arm so her luscious, full and perfectly real breasts pressed to either side of my bicep.

I swallowed hard. "You're not wearing a bra."

She smiled, the secret sort. I knew I'd love whatever fell out of her mouth next. "I'm not wearing any underwear at all. Being so perfect is so...perfectly monotonous." She lifted her chin and stared straight into my eyes, the devil in her shining through. "And I'm a dirty, dirty girl, Barclay."

I had no words, only a sense of wonder.

Perhaps I don't need to break you after all.

It looked like her flirt was out to play, and I was her full focus.

Genie's fingers fiddled with my bowtie, teasing and flicking. The air in the car diminished a fraction, and then a fraction more. *How many hours until we arrive?* I wasn't sure I'd survive at this rate. Then the tension at my throat eased, though she didn't stop her progress there. Deft fingers flicked open the top two buttons of my shirt and traced patterns on the vee of skin between.

"What if I told you this wasn't that sort of date?"

The same, secret smile, though this time she looked at them through her lashes. The movement was too practiced, but it still worked on my cock, nonetheless. "You'd be lying." Her whisper roused my blood, and nothing about that was fake at all.

"What if I told you this wasn't a pretend date after all?" My lungs constricted in time for the words to make it from my mouth. Words I wasn't sure if I wanted to take back the second my next breath made them real, but it was too late then.

"You'd still be lying."

I swore she either didn't have a skerrick of makeup on her perfect skin, or her new make-up range would be the next best product ever to come out of Rippton U.

"Is that so?" I caught her exploring fingers in a loose cage, stopping her motions before we ended up fucking like a pair of ferals in the back of my step-mother's car. "Do you know me that well?"

Despite crushing on the girl for the past full

semester, I'd barely spoken to her outside one drunken—and brief—bump and grind at a Kingsman party earlier in the year. I couldn't remember the end of the song, or even what played that night.

"Not enough. Not yet." Genie licked her lips as she toyed with my fingers. Her touch remained light, still teasing, though the slightest tremble beneath promised me that this encounter had higher stakes for her than she let on as she laced ours together.

I tipped my head down, freeing one arm to stretch out across the back of the seat. Genie pressed into my side, making it all too easy to graze my knuckles over the arch of her shoulders, back and forth over sweet, lightly floral scented skin. *A handful of hours together, and I swear I'm already addicted to her.* Perhaps she was better at this than I gave her credit for.

Or maybe I was just that out of practice. America had made me soft.

One of her pink nailed hands dropped to the buttons that she hadn't touched yet just above my waist. *Okay, so not that soft.*

"Maybe we should start with a good fuck." Otherwise, I'd never be able to think once she was in the house where I last—

I squeezed my eyes shut at the memory of too

many hands on my body, stroking and playing in all the ways that I loved most. The mere memory of *his* touch, his orchestrated night left me close to disgracing myself in the Bugatti's backseat. My eyes opened to find her watching me curiously.

"I think you're doing things in reverse, Barclay." Her tone was reproving but not without a dollop of humor.

"Probably." I squeezed her gently, trying not to inhale her scent that went straight to my head. Either one. "You're so soft. "

The driver's eyes flickered across to meet mine in the rear view mirror. I instantly had no love for the man's hard smile, or the knowledge I'd probably already tripped myself up in front of my stepmother's favorite spy. At least, the one she fucked this week in order to gain the knowledge that she thought would get her the closest to my coveted bank account. That little indiscretion would cost me a pretty bribe before I even stepped foot on the estate.

My damn estate.

Because *she* lived there under the guise that *all was well* while I let her board for free. And all because an empty seat was a powerless seat. Not that I had the time nor the inclination to wield what I had right now, which was why I opted to enroll at Rippton. My father's death gave me the perfect excuse to run away from the responsibilities I'd shirked and a place to hide my pretentious stamped behind instead of attending some Swiss Alps private college with a pack of princesses. At least at Rippton I vied for attention or not with a different variety of royalty.

Genie gave a little shimmy, rubbing that perfectly soft skin right up against me in a flurry of evidence. "I am the daughter of a cosmetics giant."

"I think it might be more than that." I pressed my forehead lightly to hers. "My family is—" I closed my mouth, trying to find the right words to convey the mess she was about to step into while not alerting the spy in our midst to my preferred sort of bitching.

"As judgmental and horrific as mine?" She grinned up at me.

I huffed a laugh and tweaked her nose for the hell of it. "You're a breath of fresh air, Genie."

"Only if you rub my bottle."

I groaned. "That was terrible. Can I beg no more genie jokes for the trip?"

"No way." She definitely wiggled her shoulders against me that time, along with some of her more natural assets. "They're my favorite. And they make people *really* uncomfortable. A girl's gotta have goals, and all."

"The Americanisms really have taken in. Your mother must love that."

The one-shouldered shrug I was getting to know was her reply. "As long as I do her bidding, she doesn't much care."

A bark left me before I could school my features. Letting a sensual smile at all the things I'd do with my new little *toy* for the weekend stretch my features, I leaned my head against the buttery leather of the backseat and pulled her onto my lap. "You're such a little hell brat, aren't you?"

"Am I?" She returned to fiddling with the remnants of my necktie again. "I prefer the image of a kitten, playing around on a fluffy blanket, and shredding all the things that she just hates that day." She stretched against me and scraped her short nails none too gently along my torso to prove her point.

Four of them, actually, that I swore I'd bear the marks of when I'd change later. Not that I minded all that much.

"Maybe we should keep that for when we're..." I wanted to say, *in the bedroom*, but despite her wonderful brand of flirting, I didn't want to presume. "Alone?" I offered instead, all too conscious of the driver's eye on her and not the road. Suddenly I wanted Genie to myself, and only myself.

Her lips pressed to my ear. "When you're balls deep to the hilt inside my pretty little pussy?" Her breath tickled the sensitive flesh at my throat, and I released a breathy little moan without realizing the sound came from me for a moment. "That's what you meant, right, Barclay? Or do you say it differently?"

I know a man who would.

But I'd banished him from my thoughts when I ran from the house last time, and left him behind, along with half of my heart, or maybe a decent part of my soul. Bringing the armor back was only a part of my penance. The rest would be paid in dealing with my mother's weeping. I was certain I could bemoan the halls at some point. But right now, the pretty little thing on my lap deserved my attention.

And when in Rome...

Or at least the French countryside.

"Something like that." *I'd love to lay you out, pleat that pretty skirt to your waist, and lap at your cunt until your cream for me, little kitten.* But I didn't know if that would be what she needed to hear... Or if my suggestion would come across as an invitation. Recovering my sanity in time—just—I slid my hand over her waist and brushed the top of her ass with my thumbs.

"Shall we make a rendezvous for my room, or yours?"

Hazel eyes glowed up at me, all luminous and glowing and perfection. "Are you setting expectations early, Barclay?"

"I'm certainly not wasting any more time. I've wanted you for longer than just a weekend's dalliance, *mon petit chou.*" I grazed my lips across her cheek to her ear, loving the way she arched naturally in my hands at the barest touch. "But the driver is a hell of a perv. I'm not above sharing, but he's not my type."

Fuck, this trip would be tough enough without a pretty little thing waiting for a good fuck between bouts in my stepmother's salon.

"*Barclay.*" Genie made an exasperated sound and sat back.

I dropped my hands, already missing the warmth of her as she slithered back into her own seat and returned to my pensive study of her. "What was that?"

She raised both my eyebrows. "You're asking me? Barclay, you're bored. You're so bored you asked me to go out on a date with you and you and can't even do it right. You. Know. Better." Genie punctuated each word with a finger jab into my chest. "And look down. You must be worse off than I imagined."

She glanced pointedly down to where her demure, powder blue knee length skirt had ridden up her bare thighs to give me a tantalizing view of her naked pussy. I could *smell her* from here. How the hell had I missed that? Maybe she was right, and a little British ennui numbed my senses. Or perhaps I was just numb all over.

She hasn't said no to my teasing before, and I took the chance she offered.

"Come back here." I crooked a finger at her, my heart pounding at the thought of a second chance at her.

Offering a tantalizing half smile she came, crawling daintily across the small space and wagging her ass in a mouthwatering tease as she crossed my lap and lay down with her pert ass, barely covered by her ruched skirt, right in my lap.

"Ohhh, so maybe you're not so bored after all." She crooked her legs so her midnight blue pumps waved about at my head height and shot me a coquettish look over her shoulder.

This weekend might be fun after all.

"Do you consider this appropriate behavior?" I added a sudden sharp tone to my voice, placing a firm hand right over her ass, feeling how bare she was through the filmy material.

Christ, I wanted to grip her the pert globes of her ass, squeeze her tight and watch her mewl and yelp. But not just yet. *Soon.*

"No, sir," she whispered back breathily. Color stained her cheeks, but she didn't break her gaze. I didn't dare raise my eyes to find the driver's face in the rear view mirror in case I fished out his tie with my hand and choked him with it. He could watch or not, but his odds of having a job tomorrow diminished by the second. "Wh– What are you going to do?"

"Do?" I stared down at her, loving the way she tensed, confused, over my lap, that she could feel how hard her little role play made me. "Why, nothing, my dear. Relax until we arrive. You can sit up then."

She swallowed, her lips parted in a pretty, strawberry heart shape. The tip of her tongue peeks out to trace a small 'o' shape the perfect size for—

Fucking tease.

"Yes, sir," she murmured demurely, facing the car door like an obedient little plaything. Her back arched a little, lifting her hips away from mine and easing the pressure on my cock.

The pervy driver was back again, watching me instead of the road. I risked it and met his hard eyes with a furious glare of my own as I pressed my hand over Genie's pert buttocks, pushing her down so she ground against me. Pleasure shot through me as I edged us both, prepared to take us to insanity and back with the slightest touch.

The snarl on the other man's lips said everything I needed to know. He wasn't getting action tonight if I didn't. I suspected there were cameras hidden in the car and Genie deserved much more than to star in her own porn show for my mother's viewing late this evening with her slimy sidepiece for hire.

The softest sigh left my little kitten's lips. For the rest of the trip we didn't speak. I held her there silently, teasing the ever loving fuck out of both of us as I stroked her hair and back. I prayed we'd get a moment together shortly after we arrived to put an end to the endless throb in my cock. But lonely nights listening to the endless fucking in the Kingsman house left me the King of Edging, and I wasn't about to embarrass myself any time soon.

At least, I didn't plan on it. Not that I would've minded, under the right set of circumstances. But that was the reason I hadn't asked her out, right? Fooling around with Genie Lockwood didn't affect my day to day my choices. In fact, I'd stayed away from her for exactly that reason. I screwed things up with my ex, Elisse, in a full blown saga of its own, and I didn't want Jeannie to just be another girl in a long line of meaningless American college conquests.

Let's put the fake *right back in my French fake chateau date.*

Because if I didn't hold to my guns, this weekend would go to hell faster than a priest in the dockside brothel.

The problem was, I liked the girl arched over my lap, panting softly as she tried not to writhe, suffering so prettily for me. We'd already played around a little too much for this weekend to return to being a pure fake date after all.

CHAPTER FOUR

CHAPTER FOUR

BARCLAY

"Monique. You are so lovely." Genie curtsied for my wicked stepmother like she was born to the position where she stood on the bottom step of my birthright. Well, one of many. "Your home is...just..." She breathed out and rolled her shoulders back, her face a perfect mask in its place just as it had been before I picked her up earlier.

Only myself and maybe the driver, who had disappeared in any case to put the car away and probably soap up for my stepmother, knew that her legs still trembled with need as she stepped gently toward my stepmonster. The older woman tittered as Genie continued her assault of sugared compliments and honed simpery.

"I have no words." This last was accompanied by Genie's softest, most genuine looking smile. Her hair shimmered in the French sun, pale, pink toned skin blooming in her own country, eclipsing everyone on the drive.

Not that Monique was likely to admit to the beauty before her, outclassed by the absence of makeup while her own was plastered across her skin with all the skill of a deplumed sparrow.

"Of course you don't. The chateau is superb, is it not, Barclay?" My stepmother descended from the top step of the building I once mistakenly called home. Her steps and extended hand made out that she did, in fact, own the place and didn't live here just because her presence suited my purposes and kept the place occupied.

I made a rude noise inside my cheek. Under her sharp eye I turned the sound into a cough at the last moment, earning myself a bemused look from the footman at the end of the row of house staff who should have known better than to react. But then,

Monique didn't know how to manage staff, because she'd never been trained to that either.

That little secret we kept to ourselves, of course. She couldn't admit she only played house by the grace of the stepson who neither cared about her, the land or the title, nor that she had no income nor investments of her own.

Monique caressed Genie's soft cheek with a brittle hand. Her curved, sharpened talons displayed a shade that aimed for blood but didn't quite make it. "Americans just don't have culture like we do here on the Continent."

Genie's shoulders stiffened. I doubted her tension came from the contact, or at least, not only. I caught the slight shift, so minute it was almost imperceptible, because I knew to look for the change.

Prepared for intervention as someone had once done for me, I stepped forward. My wallet was a whole lot emptier as I moved away from where the Bugatti had left us out the front of my old home, and its unpleasant, greedy driver.

"I see you two have met." I tucked Genie's hair behind her ear and pressed a kiss to the hollow of her throat, speaking softly into her ear. "You have a wet spot on the back of your skirt. Small, but telling." I licked her skin, grateful for my prior local reputation as a Lothario that cloaked my true nature to perfection.

She slid her hand beneath the one I curved over her stomach and scratched my palm with those mini talons of her own while the stepmonster watched on with the sort of green tinged vitriol in her eyes that left me semi hard at her pathetic efforts. *Too fucking cute.* I laughed softly into Genie's ear, pulling her into my body so her curves found all the right pressure points for both of us, if I measured her soft not-quite gasp well.

"Can't keep your hands to yourself can you, Barclay." My stepmother actually clapped her hands to get our attention as though we were kindergarteners.

I gazed up at her like the lovelorn teen I'd never been. My dopey grin instantly lowered the IQ of the household staff lining the drive who deserved far better.

From the corner of my eye, someone tall shifted. The faintest snicker reached me—again, I was sure, by design. My heart pounded a little harder in my chest as I forced my gaze to stay steady on the step-monster.

"Good to see you've kept the place in order in my absence, Monica." I mispronounced her name for the pure, perverse pleasure of seeing her over Botoxed eyes attempt to widen in outrage, and fail. "Shall we?"

I kissed the corner of Genie's mouth as she continued to blush oh so fucking beautifully and led her up the stairs with a general nod to the gathered contingent of staff. Many seemed to have survived the purge Monique made of decimating the place the day my father passed and I left in an attempt to leave her mark on La Borde.

A week later, I hired them all back with instructions they could only be let go under extreme circumstances...and with my signature, made in hand before my local *avocat* or equivalent. A phone call or eight I enjoyed far too much. The stepmonster loved that little tweak, and painted the entire bottom level of the house in revenge in a truly disgusting shade called *poached salmon.*

I changed the carpets to an equally hideous and clashworthy cyan shag pile in nylon that I ripped straight out of a seventies retro warehouse I was almost certain had been used as a porn casting studio. As an extra, I also gave every single employee an early Christmas bonus worth double their wage for dealing with her, every year.

And I'd halved Monique's allowance.

Permanently.

In the end it was her loss—she had to stare at that carpet and walk on it every day. I didn't. When I called, the horrendous color scheme reminded me to maintain my battles in the most petty fashion possible and to always tip my waiter extravagantly and with a kiss behind closed doors.

Or to occasionally forget to close them at all.

That way, any spit in my eggs was well paid spit.

"You are the limit," Genie whispered under her breath, trembling in her attempt to contain her giggles.

We passed beyond the etched, folding glass windows of the entrance way that would never have held in any incursion in any decade. That entrance was a pure indulgence, nothing more. The chateau was less of a castle and more an extravagance of the highest tier. Those windows that doubled as the building's entrance were gilt in actual gold. A matching Louis V painted fresco ceiling decorated the ceiling above us that the monster thankfully hadn't been able to ruin.

"Maybe." I shrugged, rolling my shoulders back to ease the familiar growing tension and collection of knots accumulated there. "But that is a pretty wet spot on your skirt."

Her cheeks glowed brighter than ever. I grinned, catching her hand in mine to raise our laced fingers to my lips.

"Sir. Shall I have your bags brought to your usual rooms?" A deep voice echoed along the empty foyer hall. "And the armor in its cases?"

I closed my eyes and squeezed Genie's hand tight without looking back. Too tight.

I did see him.

My voice obeyed me when I opened my mouth by some blessed miracle, holding my own facade up for the barest minutes when I needed the world to perform to my whim away, even away from the eyes of others.

Only before the ones who mattered to me most, at least in this moment.

"Yes, Jacques. That would be lovely. Thank you. Who will be looking after Genie? I sent word to the — To Monique that she would accompany me." I only stumbled once, but fortunately this was company where I could stutter and stammer all I liked.

Because he liked it when I floundered.

Flushed. Became flustered.

When I stumbled and couldn't hold myself together when he—

Fuck, not here.

I couldn't let those memories hit me here or I wouldn't make it past the damned foyer.

"I believe she is letting her own maid look after your...friend, sir," Jacques murmured the picture of pure etiquette and decorum as always.

Genie swallowed, looking up at me when my hand flexed on her waist. *Former lover?* she mouthed.

Her comment made more sense now. Perhaps this was how I behaved around a certain Rippton U dark prince when he flirted, too. Though Jacques hadn't exactly started flirting. I'd be on my damn knees if that happened, and—

Damnit.

I gave her an imperceptible nod, knowing my features were too strained. My throat tightened. All I wanted was to rake a hand over my face and douse myself in the fountain out the front. Actually, that wasn't such a bad idea. Maybe I should.

Genie flashed me a flirtatious, imp like smile. She spun on her heel, took the decision right out of my hands and placed it squarely in hers. "I know I'm breaking all the rules but us Yanks can do that, can't we?" My petite little kitten threw on a thick

Southern accent and sashayed her way straight at Jacques.

My six and a half foot tall ex-lover flinched. I didn't blame him.

"Genie," I admonished her softly. Sweetly.

In reality I was delighted to see someone other than myself raise hell in a life I should be living but refused to have.

She shot me the bird behind her back and sauntered right up to Jacques, placing her hand in the middle of his chest. He never moved as she toyed with the buttons on his shirt the way she had done to mine in the car. The man swung both ways as much as I did, though that was because in his place and with his looks, guests expected it of him. He had trained himself to want women but I knew he preferred men. That practiced little move, however...

My eyes narrowed, and Jacques caught the expression before I could erase it from my face.

"My services are to my lord," he murmured, using the tips of his fingers to push her pale wrists away with his much larger hands. His head lowered and he hissed sharply in her ear just loud enough for me to catch his words from a dozen paces away. "I don't do females."

Genie beamed up at him and didn't back off an

inch. "Then I guess we're sharing." She held her pose a moment longer, then leaned further forward into the alpha male's space and flicked invisible lint from his sleeve. "I suppose we'll see you up there?" She waited for a name my frozen valet seemed unlikely to ever provide.

"Jacques," I said helpfully, sliding one hand into my pocket. I adjusted myself at the impossible show playing out before me.

Hells, seeing the two of them going at it made for the perfect sex sandwich... If I could talk either of them into sharing a space after this.

"Jacques," she purred, trailing her fingers along his breastbone through his pristine white shirt. "You know, if I didn't know better, I'd say you were a liar." His eyes narrowed as his gaze left me and focused on her. She giggled, dropping her hands, and shrugged. "But that's okay. I am too."

She swiveled on her heel like a catwalk model and sauntered back to me, looping her hand through my elbow. Genie chattered softly at my side about nothing at all as she towed me up the stairs without missing a beat. I steered her in the right direction, my mouth agape at how well she'd pissed off the one person in the household that it was almost impossible to get a rise out of.

"What did you just do, you little hellion?" I murmured, still in awe of her skills and more than a little aroused.

"Nothing." She gave me wide eyes and flicked her tongue at the corner of her mouth. "He is fun. I see why you like him."

I stopped at the corner of the hallway that led to my wing of the house. "You're not jealous?"

She laughed, a musical sound that wound its way through the scarred holes in my soul. "No, Barclay. Why should I? It's fake, remember?" Genie turned in a circle, frowning at the plethora of doors that all appeared the same and down an identical hallway branching off the first. "Is it this way?" She pointed down the hall.

"Not like it was when I offered," I muttered. "Third on the left," I called out as a broad, strong hand slipped around my waist from behind, pulling me into an empty study reserved for my private use.

I yanked at the too-tight collar of my shirt as Jacques shut the door and flicked the lock, a hungry expression on his face.

"I've missed you, my lord," he whispered, stalking forward.

His hands framed my face and his mouth crashed down. My ex-lovers kiss was violent and dominating as I remembered. A large hand gripped my thickening cock through my trousers as he worked me hard. Guilt bombarded me. For the first time ever I had to drown the urge to push out of Jacques's arms and run after Genie.

Fake. It's all fake.

Every second of it.

Nothing about this is real. He wants a job. He wants a raise. He wants–

Me.

Lie, lie, lie.

Ah, fuck it.

Another thing I drowned in as Jacques's hand slid inside my slacks and pumped me roughly enough that I was ready to spill seconds later.

It doesn't matter.

She approves.

A deep groan built in my throat. Jacques's mouth found mine again as he grabbed a wad of tissues and stuffed them inside my pants seconds before I disgraced myself. I sagged in his arms with a groan I felt to the tingling curve of my emptied ball sack.

"I've missed you," he murmured, nuzzling my throat as he cleaned me tenderly, and dropped to his knees.

The sight of him below me was too much, and my cock hardened again at his siren call.

I shouldn't—

She doesn't care—

And with Jacques's eyes on mine as he took the head of my cock between his lips, cleaning and sucking me at once. I let all thought of Genie, my guilt, and everything else dissipate as I sank into the pure pleasure of the sort of worship only this man could give who knew every secret and every desire I possessed.

The man I'd left behind and shattered his heart so long ago.

The man who knelt for me now.

And as I laced my hands through the dominant valet's hair, working myself against his throat as I moaned, I knew I had to both trust him, and not. Because I'd broken his heart and run from him once before.

And Jacques never forgot.

Or forgave.

CHAPTER FIVE

JACQUES

I pretended not to care about the girl that the man I loved had brought home with him for the first time in nearly three years. I pretended not to care about the girl he hadn't fucked in the back of his stepmother's car, though it had been a close thing from how both of them clung to each other as they escaped Monique's talons at the top of the house's steps.

And I pretended not to care about the way Barclay's hands clawed needily at my hair as he came in my mouth. My lord pulled me onto his cock with the sort of strangled sigh that told me he hadn't been taking care of himself the way I made him promise the day he left La Borde. The day of his father's funeral when I made him promise that he would take care of himself when I wasn't there to do it for him.

And from the way my lord tumbled forward over me as I wiped my hand across my mouth after licking him clean, then gently tucked him back into his silk and wool blend pants, I knew one thing with absolute certainty:

My lord was a liar.

And that would never be alright.

The term I used for him wasn't the correct one for our kind, but we had never played by society's rules. A tongue in cheek name I'd given him when I first arrived at the house to fullfil a different set of duties before I became his valet a year later and we fell in love. Or I thought we had. Then he left, and I wasn't so sure.

I straightened around Barclay's slumped, panting form, stroking his hair. Sweat beaded his forehead. I brushed the moisture back into his hairline, holding his slight physique to my chest. Barclay Augustus Chesterfield might be a giant compared to the slip of a female who he had brought home to play with all weekend, but next to me, he barely came to my shoulder.

I leaned down and licked across his temple,

suppressing a moan. "Thank you, my lord," I murmured, tucking him against me as I used the honorific that used to be a humiliation for him that became a pet name over time when we played together. "Do you need me to take you to your room?"

Barclay always preferred courtesy, and formality. If he didn't want that, he told me as much directly. And in his home, I played by his rules. On the rare occasion we were out, away from this place, we played by mine.

"Christ, I've missed you," he whispered, pulling away from me to swipe a trembling hand across his face.

I frowned. The hollows beneath his eyes were deeper than I'd initially thought. "Are you sleeping at all?" I snapped, catching his jaw. Turning his face side to side, I studied the sallow color of his skin. Hell, his eye sockets were on show giving him a skeletal look. "What is that holiday that you Americans like so much, All Hallows?"

"Halloween," Barclay muttered, suppressing a yawn. "It's nearly evening, Jacques. Genie will need dinner."

I glanced at the window and frowned. "The sun is still up, *my lord*," I said pointedly. "Dinner will not be served until after nine." *As you should remember.*

"Christ." He yawned again. "Neither of us will make it that long. Can we eat in our rooms? Together?" He looked longingly at the door.

A spike of anger lanced through my gut. "Did you come all the way back here," I asked my voice low. "Just to eat *in your rooms?*" My rage was barely concealed and completely inappropriate for our relationship—either of them—considering my status, but Barclay appeared too distracted or exhausted to register my emotional opinion on the matter.

Or perhaps he just didn't care.

The Barclay I remembered cared. A fucking lot. He found every staff member in the house and he knew their names. Their stories. He talked to them about their family. He knew the history of this place. Of the people who worked here. Who made La Borde their life.

A life he was supposed to live. And then he walked away.

From me. From all of us.

"Do you need me to—" I tried again, my mouth snapping shut when he waved a hand in dismissal.

"I'm fine. Thank you." Barclay had always been good at distancing himself when required.

Me, not so much.

I watched my lord as he walked away from me for the second time in nearly three years, from almost the same situation. He stumbled, placed one hand against a wall that wasn't where he remembered it.

This time, I wasn't there to catch him.

He looked back as he recovered himself on a nearby chair.

Once, a pretty red flush would have stained the English cheeks I hated when I first met the young lord before I fell in love with the man with the huge heart.

Once, he would have panted for me when I covered his cock with my hand over his pants and stroked him to a delicious, humiliating ruined orgasm that we both craved from him.

Today was nothing like that.

Now, I stood back and let him stumble. Let him fall. Made him recover on his own.

And his cheeks remained pale.

"Are you alright, my lord?" I asked, always the courteous valet as required.

Because in his absence I, too, had become a master of distance. Learned its sharp sting. The ache of an ocean between us. Begged him to return. Back then, I broke all the rules.

And received...

Nothing. Nothing at all for any of my efforts.

And so that's what I gave him now. A void of emptiness that yawned between us.

Barclay straightened, inclining his head. The perfect mask of man I knew back in place. Everything about him was so fucking *fake, fake, fake*.

"Thank you, Jacques. I am...fine."

I smiled at his back as he walked through the gilded, powder blue doors that matched the walls of the blue room in the Monaco palace.

My lord, the liar.

But you can't lie to me forever.

Even if he could, apparently, lie to himself.

CHAPTER SIX

BARCLAY

Jacques held out my dinner jacket. Gray eyes traveled over my body. Not a word slipped from his lips of what we'd done earlier, or how I walked away. As always, he remained the epitome of discretion.

I followed that lead, slipping my arms into the garment and tried to ignore his presence as he worked on my cufflinks. Neither of us had spoken since I stepped out of the shower to find him in my room, presenting me with two dinner options after I'd slept off the ex-lover hangover of epic proportions. All after he'd made me lose control not just once, but twice within half an hour of arriving at La Borde.

One long finger traced across my pulse point, lingering across my bare flesh. My heart rate ratcheted up a notch, and I knew we both understood just what sort of power Jacques still held over me. I snarled my discontent at him, and reached out to do my own buttons, but he batted my hands away.

"You've forgotten how things are done here, my lord." He shook his head, making a mockery of my own attempt to dress myself. Talented fingers slid each button together in an out of order dressing that left his hands skating over my bare skin on my torso as often as possible. Jacques reached around my waist to tuck the shirt into my pants at the back, his chest almost pressed against mine.

Almost.

The man was a study of decorum, but also a master of control and flirtation. He could wring a tease out for hours, days.

Fucking weeks until I crawled and begged for what only he could offer.

We both knew that.

Only, this time, I didn't have weeks at hand for him to fine tune his greatest weapon.

"I can put those on myself, " I said dryly. "America hasn't changed me quite so much."

Liar.

He didn't need to say it. I read the truth in his gray eyes. Jacques stood a good head above me. His shoulders were wider, too. The man could flatten me if he so chose, and for good reason. Rather than tip my head back the way he wanted so our mouths aligned, the perfect height for kissing or spitting—*Christ, how many times had he done either of those things to me?*—I focused my gaze a little lower after risking a glance upward without moving my chin.

A mistake, as that left me staring at his arched mouth that had kissed me so roughly I'd come in his hand hours before. My cock jerked to attention in my pants and I closed my eyes, trying to refocus but nothing seemed to work.

"Perhaps it has." Jacques finished with my buttons. "You have changed, my lord. Perhaps too much."

I didn't bother to answer though I knew I should berate him, put him back in his place. But I didn't have the energy to fight when I still had dinner with Monique to go. And Genie...

"Fuck," I muttered, neither aiming the curse at him or myself.

Instead, I let him manhandle me, looking out at the darkened hedge illuminated by lamp posts that studded walk that decorated the entire front of the house where this bedroom looked over. The greenery formed a seasonal labyrinth beyond my window.

A perfect place for midnight rendezvous, a child's imagination or to walk straight into the middle should one know the way and have the desire to scream themselves silly.

"Did we confirm which maid was assigned to Genie? Monique has..."

Specific taste in her spies.

I wasn't so sure on Genie's aptitude about intrigue, though she must be reasonably business savvy. But there was a difference between a board-room and a French salon. Both were savage places where a word held several meanings. Not that she was a stranger to our language by any means, nor probably as half as out of practice as me. But I hadn't had a chance to warn her before Jacques accosted me before, either, or when I crashed afterward.

I only wished it had been in their arms.

Either of them.

Both.

"I didn't check who Monique sent to her." Jacques pulled my belt from around the back of his neck, snapping the leather between us. "I'm sure we will find out shortly. You may rearrange the house-hold as you see fit."

"Bullshit." I didn't so much as flinch when he snapped the leather, though it annoyed me that he lied to my face.

The man knew everything that happened on the estate. But we both knew that any chances I made her this weekend would simply be changed back the moment I drove back to the airport and my *other* life.

So far, the only staff that had spoken to me was Jacques. The rest were either feeling their way along to who I'd become, didn't trust me any longer, or the step monster had threatened them unsuitably before I stepped over the threshold.

I voted for a heady mixture of the last two.

Thank fuck I'll be out of here in just over forty-eight hours.

"Probably." Jacques answers my unspoken sentiment, reading my mind, as always. Another skill I admired in him. His talent to be able to read a room and slide into conversation anywhere. It was as though I were the unskilled one, and him the *courtier* in this situation. He pressed the button on my pants, and finished tucking my shirt in, pleating the folds meticulously.

I closed my eyes at the sensation of his hands on me, remembering the last time we were together, before I left. How his palm gripped firmly around my throat, his cock lodged deep inside me while I dampened the sheets beneath us with my sweat, cum and tears.

"I enjoyed making you come, my lord." Jacques's fingers brushed over my cock. My eyes drifted shut at the reminder. Still lost in my memories, I hardened beneath the silk blend of my pants as he tugged at my fly. He stopped halfway, and my eyes fluttered open. "Did I catch on something?" he asked, quietly.

My cock throbbed against the knuckles that nestled just inside my pants as he worked the zipper, rubbing up and down a few times.

The world dimmed the edges as I stared at him. "Perhaps you'd best take a closer look."

"I'm not sure it needs quite that, my lord." His affection, the way he spoke to me, sent my body into an arch as he rubbed his fingertips over the front of my pats. Fuck, he'd ruin me before I left for dinner at this rate. Jacques's smile sharpened. He knelt, slowly bringing his face level with my crotch. "Perhaps there's a thread caught."

Any other time I would've laughed at his audacity, but his touch had me so fucking ready to blow. *Again.*

And I hadn't done anything for him yet.

"I'd rather not leave a mess where anyone can see

it," I said, keeping my face as expressionless as possible.

We both knew this game. If someone came in and saw us, he'd be sacked and would leave the residence without a reference. Another job with a family of repute would be beyond difficult for him to achieve at that point.

Monique excelled at destroying others, reveled in it.

He ran his knuckles along the length of my cock as I hardened painfully inside the slowly closing confines of my pants. "I think I've got it," he said, softly.

I stared straight down at him. My voice hardened, though I kept my volume low. "Use your teeth."

Jacques dropped his hands and leaned forward, gently taking my zip in his teeth and drew it upward. When he reached the absolute top, he worked the flap over my zip, concealing the majority of my arousal and pressed dry kiss against my crotch, tracing his fingertips lightly over my shape until an unwilling moan tore from my lips. "Welcome home, my lord."

Once more, maybe twice, and I'd ruin everything he just fixed.

Or maybe that had been his goal all along.

Sensation fanned through my crotch, heating my concealed flesh until even the jacket felt too damn tight. I allowed the corner of my mouth to flick up. "I think the last time I was here I was screaming, and you were lodged inside my ass."

"But that game has two doors." He pressed his mouth to my crotch again and kissed my aching cock.

I allowed another soft groan to tumble from my lips just as the door to my room opened. *I should have fucking locked it.* But instead of the alarm I felt registering in his eyes, disappointment washed over his features. I only had a brief glimpse before I spun away, flicking the button of my jacket over the damp mark he left as the only evidence of our favorite playtime.

"Christ and heaven, Barclay. You have your manservant picking up lint off the floor. We have maids for that sort of rubbish. Overpaying for his services. I've always said..." my stepmother ranted, her lip curling upward.

I closed my eyes against every response to that sexist remark, strangling the back of the vanity chair and wished it was her throat. "Monique. I thought we were meeting you downstairs?"

My stepmother invaded the space behind us, turning about the room until her back stood to me in an overt denial of the etiquette the bitch apparently clung to. Jacques risked a glance upward, the faintest hint of a smile brushing his lips before he climbed to his feet and turned away, the picture of the perfect, subservient valet.

Who he had never been.

My heart ripped at the sight. All I wanted to do was launch myself at him and promise he was free to behave as he wanted.

In our world, that still wasn't always the case.

Jacques watched me for a moment longer from his stilled position. Whatever he read of my body language hardened his face. A second later he removed himself from the room while I tried to regulate my breathing, his phantom touch both a tease and an absolute necessity for my survival.

"Celeste is looking after Genevieve." Monique dallied at the dresser, and then approached me with the bottle of cologne. "Your father loved this one. You should wear it."

Her words could be construed as caring and at worst condescending. But her pale, almost colorless green eyes reminded me of a viper in the nest.

"I shouldn't leave her alone too long. After all, she is American." The pretty lie Genie created and that I now fostered sat easy on my tongue.

Monique raised the bottle, her finger on the pump. I twisted away before she could spray the horrific smelling odour on my skin, desperate to retain Jacques's faint scent of midnight illicit kisses despite that we hadn't struck the appropriate hour yet. *But we will.*

None of us would sleep much tonight, I expected, not with how Genie had declared herself earlier.

But Monique, always the pushy, inappropriate bitch, stalked forward and attacked me with the bottle.

I froze in place, not allowing my fists to clench or my shoulders to tighten as I became a Barclay shaped statue beneath the glittery spray of nothing my father ever chose to wear.

All I smelled was an excess of cheap bullshit bearing a brand Monique purchased on his behalf. Every spray erased one more memory from his home. My home.

Until everything around us was hers.

Hers, hers, hers.

Sprayed with shitty perfume most likely purchased at a discount sale.

Monique pointed her bleached incisors in my

direction, "There, that's better, don't you think? Now, your father can be with us all night."

"You make it sound like you had his ashes dropped into the thing." My gaze dropped to the swirling, purple liquid in its elegant cushion cut bottle, but no evidence of my father's interment was visible inside its glass prison.

I wouldn't put it past her.

"You've become so American." Monique *tsked* at me, sounding more British by the moment. A chameleon if there ever was one.

"You'd know, stepmother. You were born there." I clicked my heels together against the floor, wishing like Dorothy to return home, and maybe take Genie and Jacques with me.

I was still recovering from seeing him again, figuring that after a few years of absence he would have sought employment—and love—elsewhere.

"That was a long time ago."

"Yes, because you're so old."

She clucked her tongue at me, her eyes narrowing, fake smile spread wide. "Come now." She slotted her hand through my elbow, manipulating me like a boxed toy into the shape she preferred. "Our guests will be waiting."

I didn't look at her as she towed me towards the door. "I thought it was just family."

Her laughter dribbled down my spine in an unpleasured and far too intimate contact. "Whoever said that?"

You did, you time waste of a fucking liar.

A smile that barely hid her proverbial fangs was the only answer the wicked witch gave as I allowed her to drag me to my fate.

CHAPTER SEVEN

BARCLAY

"Tonight is going to be an utter disaster."

I cupped Genie's chin. When her lips parted for a kiss, I dribbled a mouthful of expensive family labeled chardonnay between them.

The ballroom was full of guests I didn't know and for that, more was the far more fucking merrier. Because if I was going to self-implode, I'd do it publicly and in style.

The worst of it was that I still didn't understand why I had hauled my pasty ass partway around the globe to find out what Monique wanted...because she wouldn't tell me. So far I'd been shown off in front of her friends, introduced to neighbors I didn't know I had, and simpered over by a cache of Parisian girls shipped in for the occasion.

Genie saved me from that conundrum of actually telling the poor things that I was taken on two fronts and that they'd just have to make do with the very well hung stable boy around the back, assuming that Vincent still worked for us and that Monique hadn't banished him from the property yet. Doubtful, if she'd discovered his particular oral skills that he backed up with stunning enthusiasm and endless stamina.

The concept of doing the decorous thing and leaving deserted me hours ago, around the time of the first course at Monique's long dinner table. That was when the woman next to me decided to have a grope beneath my napkin, no doubt in a bid to secure an emergency pregnancy that would lead to a child of semi noble birth that didn't really count on this country, or some other such rubbish.

I was inclined to give her my American body count just to see the horror written across the face that I'd end up reading as tomorrow's Parisian headline proclaiming my playboy status and unchanged French tendencies.

Then every whore and its pussy would be after

the foppish cock I pretended to be—mostly—and I'd never get enough peace to fuck either Genie or Jacques. Or perhaps both of them together.

A decanter of red wine spilled over the offending guest shortly afterwards, and Jacques ushered her to a bathroom. I hadn't seen my attacker as my valet fulfilled his secondary, or what that his primary task, whisking away any threat to my personage.

Which brought me back to Genie bent backward in my arms, trying not to let the sweet and sour wine I dribbled into her mouth spill down her cheeks. A game we played where my breath holding skills outmatched hers, apparently. Perhaps we could put that to the test later.

Her eyes widened as she swallowed frantically, desperate to play by my rules—I was grateful, and half hard—as I toyed with her in front of an entire ballroom of my stepmother's peers.

Read that one carefully. My stepmonster's peers, *not* mine.

Which meant I got to play bad, be filthy and absolutely, ten thousand percent, *not* give a flying fuck what a single one of them thought of my behavior whatsoever.

Especially when Jacques, doubling for a waiter this evening in all white with a black bow tie and bearing a fresh tray of champagne to mix my drinks nicely, topped me up for round two.

"In case of your need, sir," he murmured almost reverently. Dark eyes glowed at me over the tray of bubbles while Genie choked prettily on my saliva in my arms.

Across the room, Monique and her friends *tksed* and *ahhed* like the fucking British, utterly disgracing themselves while I flirted and played with two lovers at once.

France is good for me.

I couldn't deny it as Genie reached through the enormous folds of the ball gown she managed to compress into an overnight case by some miracle. The voluminous skirts hid her otherwise obvious grope. She played with my balls through my suit pants while Jacques turned a pretty shade of lily pad green.

I laughed softly, holding his gaze. Tonight couldn't be more perfect.

Taking the chilled champagne with a steady hand, I tipped a little of the fresh golden liquid between Genie's lips. She swallowed sweetly, the tip of her tongue flicking out to catch a drop that beaded on her lip.

"Delightful," I murmured, as she fluttered her lashes. "And cheeky."

"Should I be any other way?" Genie adjusted my bowtie, a pale pink that matched the scalloped lace on her rose gold gown.

"Sir." Jacques circled us and discreetly tugged at the neckline of Genie's dress where it pulled down to expose the dusky top of her nipple on one side.

The heated glance that seared the air between them left me light headed. *There is hope.* I wrapped my arm tighter around Genie's waist as a few caustic members of Monique's posse appeared on either side of us.

I was sure they meant to appear imposing, but Genie *just* managed to repress a giggle as their strategic appearance, her face pinking prettily with each stifled breath.

"Can I help you, ladies?" I asked, letting my Parisian accent thicken, but spoke in English all the same, just to be a pest.

"Oh, Barclay. Don't you know how much better a French woman is in bed?" One woman with a head full of ringlets that belonged firmly in the previous century or the one before that murmured, dancing a little closer on heels that left her tottering.

"Or two, or three." Daphne, a dark haired Medusa simpered from Genie's other side.

"Oh, do tell, ladies. I'm always up for a little education." Genie winked at me.

I sipped my champagne and said nothing.

"Well, a French woman uses her tongue on... everything," Daphne proclaimed, aiming, I suspected for shock value.

"And she always...swallows," her counterpart offered as Genie finished her flute, timing the comment to perfection.

Still, Rippton had better seductresses than this lot, and as Genie pinned me earlier in the day, I was bored.

"Mademoiselles," I murmured. "If my step-mother wanted to marry me off to the local courtesan faction, all she has to do is ask." Both women stared at me with a renewed speculative fervor in their eyes. Even Genie watched me with a degree of caution. I smiled broadly. "The answer will always be a resounding 'no'. Goodnight." I nodded to them and drew Genie out of the ostentatious, stifling ballroom.

My breath came a little harder as we hit the stairs. I stopped, gripping the banister tight.

"Are you alright, Barclay?" Genie laid a hesitant hand on my sleeve. "I know this isn't a real date, but if you need to talk, I'm a blank ear. Your secrets have nowhere to go. I don't know these people, nor do I care about any of them."

Her blush pink lips parted as if she would say more but the longer I waited, the more strained the silence between us became.

"I don't doubt it." I sighed and raked a hand through my hair, mucking up the styling but it wasn't like it mattered in this place. "I can't deal with being back here. My father, mother... They've been erased from this place. I never should have let her stay. Monique, I mean." *As if there's any doubt about* who. "We're only here because I needed to make an overdue appearance that I've avoided for the past two years plus, electing to spend my hours in the US and ignore my responsibilities to these people." I gestured to the staff with their stiff backs and starched uniforms floating about and serving as needed.

Like Jacques, here without me all this time.

Anger burned within me that he stayed. Damnit, why *did* he stay? Out of some misplaced sense of loyalty? Hope? So much good it's done him. I'd bet everything I have that the last years under Monique's reign have been anything but prosperous. Only the ironclad contracts myself and my father's lawyer drew up kept her from pilfering everything.

"Fucking gold digger," I muttered. "Not you," I added hastily when Genie raised a querying eyebrow.

"They look...neutral," Genie said carefully after a moment's thought, apparently electing to ignore my outburst. "They don't appear unhappy exactly, but also I don't believe that they're okay with how she manages them. And she must be crippling your bank account with this bullshit, unless you have guidance in place for that, too."

I smiled. Genie read the situation perfectly within seconds. *There's that business brain in play that I knew I would love.* "Indeed. Now tell me how you managed to get that gown into your pretty little carry on? Is it bigger on the inside?"

Genie gave me a startled laugh. "Nerd. And the bag, or the dress?"

"Clever girl." I leaned down to kiss her in full. Soft lips parted beneath my urgency, letting me in as pure desire shot through me in an instant hit of a drug bearing her name. I slid my tongue along hers, seeking some assurance I wasn't alone in this catastrophe of a visit. "May I take you upstairs, Miss Lockwood?"

Genie pulled back, breathless. "Are you asking, Barclay? Or demanding?"

I bared my teeth. "Tell me what you need and I'll provide it as a thank you for dealing with my family bullshit, and mine."

"What I need is to see you happy." Her hazel gaze searched mine.

I drew back, dropping my hands. The moment I released her, I felt empty. An abyss fell between us that I dared not cross. Or was too cowardly.

"That's not how this works," I said, slightly unsteady on my heeled boots. "We agreed it was pretend."

"I'm human, Barclay," she said with no small amount of exasperation. "I care about the man kissing me."

"Not the deal," I snapped, and sucked in a long breath. "Can I tuck you in? I might go for a walk."

Across the fields, into the forest. Over the river and never stop.

Or enter the labyrinth and scream myself hoarse, as I'd done a dozen times or more before.

If I cupped my hands over my mouth, I'd learned those screams couldn't be heard from the house. Otherwise, more than one person lied to me.

Genie's chin tipped up, her cheeks flushing, and

not in the way I liked. Her eyes glossed with a sheen of unshed misery. "I can find the way to my room, thank you my lord." She fucking curtsied flawlessly for me and darted up the stairs like Cinderella running from the ball.

Only I wasn't the one left holding a glass slipper. I glanced around for Jacques's support, but he was nowhere in sight. Hell, I was left holding nothing at all, only my battered pride in the house I was born in, feeling so out of place after my absence that I wished I'd never come home at all.

Lie.

Swearing not so quietly, I strode into the nearest small study and grabbed a decanter of some flavored alcohol that could have been pure poison for all I knew. My head still spun with Genie's denial and my own frustration on so many fronts. I headed out the glassed front entrance of the house without recognizing the doormen standing on either side with the intent of obliterating myself deep in the estate's labyrinth.

My two chosen points for this evening's entertainment.

Which is what I did, right until the sun began to crest in a pale sky.

* * *

Breakfast—officially brunch as the household never did rise before midday, particularly after an event—was over before I made my way back into the house, unbuttoning my shirt that itched with last night's sweat. Maybe some other things. My breaths came short with the need to get rid of it *now* as I winced at the excess of fucking sunlight *everywhere*. I'd been happier under the hedge I'd woken beneath, but the ants decided I was their breakfast, and I reluctantly moved along.

I peeled the shirt off as I managed to hold my shit together long enough to walk up the stairs rather than run to my wing like a toddler, though I did throw the offending garment at my bed where Jacques magically appeared to collect the sweat stained material before it hit the coverlet.

"Would you like a—" he started.

I never found out what he was offering as I walked into the ensuite and threw the shower on as cold as it would go. Stepping in while I was still discarding my pants and shoes, I tossed them in a damp heap in one corner, letting cold water cascade over my back.

Its icy prickles soothed me.

Slowly, the itchiness subsided. I breathed in deeply for the first time in what felt like hours and rested my hands on the cold tiles above my head.

"My lord. Is there anything—" Jacques appeared in the doorway I hadn't shut.

Nor had I expected my newfound peace to be interrupted.

"Get out," I snapped coldly, hating the disturbance that stole my sense of solitude. "I don't need you today."

Silence reigned for a full, strained minute. The bathroom door shut gently, and I was alone.

"Fuck," I grated under my breath, slamming my palm into the tiles, over and over until they stung. "Fuck, fuck, *fuck*."

But I'd dismissed him, and as a good valet, Jacques took me at my word and left.

I swallowed hard and tipped my head back into the icy spray, relishing the sharp pin pricks that tortured my skin. The pain offered a particular brand of a distraction against the loneliness swirling in my chest.

I hate this fucking place. And maybe some of the people in it.

Including myself.

CHAPTER EIGHT

GENIE

I wanted to flounce about my room, pound and throw things, but I had something more productive in mind. And I knew just the man to help me get it.

Jacques should have been dressing Barclay after he stumbled in from the garden sometime around midday. Like everyone, I sleep long, if not well. The bedding was comfortable and I wasn't cold, but I wished I'd been able to fall asleep with Barclay, or that I'd followed him the night before. But after I ran back to my room, I'd lost sight of him and I knew nothing about the estate or the house that seemed to grow corridors and turn after turn of duplicate doors, enough to become a horror film in its own right.

The flirtatious man of the night before was not the one who returned this morning. I knew that even Jacques followed him into his rooms and shut the door behind them both. It was on the tip of my tongue to tell him not to push Barclay, but then they seemed to have a history and at this point I suspected he knew Barclay a whole hell of a lot more than I did.

I loitered near Barclay's rooms in the hope of catching him after taking my breakfast in my bed when it was offered. I mean, what girl turns that down after crying herself to sleep the night before? But the person I caught coming out of Barclay's rooms wasn't the man I sought.

It was Jacques.

The valet turned ex turned lover strode away along the hall with the sort of determination that promised distance between them

Which was the sort of distraction I also required this morning. Perhaps we could be of use to each other. Either way, he wouldn't get a chance to say *no*. Not with me.

"I need to shoot something." I fell into step beside him. Not an easy feat when his legs seemed twice as long as long as mine, and his stride worked at double my speed. I kept up, even when he shook his head decisively.

"No, you don't."

"Yes, I do," I countered. "You know that if I don't get you to agree, then I'll just find someone else to show me where everything is kept, load up and go out and do it on my own anyway." I didn't bother turning that statement into a prettily phrased question. We both knew I'd do it.

Jacques sighed but his pace slowed. "How long has it been since you've shot?" he growled.

"Too long," I admitted. "But I'm sure I remember where everything goes." I let the ramifications of that sink in for a moment. "Or you could just come with me, torture—I mean, tutor me, and then let me do my thing."

Jacques said nothing for a long moment. Actually, I didn't think he breathed at all. Finally, he made a sound that resembled two cars crashing. If I hadn't been prepared for some level of drama llama activity, I would have been alarmed.

Instead, I looked up at him. "So, are we sharing now?" I asked brightly.

Jacques stopped and glared at me. "No. We are

not, 'sharing now,' he mimicked me cruelly, laughing when I rocked back a half step. If I hadn't been prepared already, the sound would have actually frightened me. "You should be running, American girl. Run far from me, as far as you can. I can't control your new boyfriend, nor can I save him from himself. Do you understand that? He's going to come apart this weekend. Right. Fucking. Here. And there's nothing he'll let me do about it." Jacques stared at me. Short breaths panted from his lips, his heavy chest heaving.

And all I wanted to do was wrap my arms around his waist and hold him.

I don't do women.

He said that to me yesterday. I thought it was yesterday. My hours were already running together.

"I understand," I murmured.

Jacques glared at me. "No, you don't."

"Don't I?' I laughed, a brittle horrible sound. "I came here as your boyfriend's fake date. The fake date I've wanted for so long and when he did ask me out it was...wrong. Meaningless. But I said yes because I was curious. I wanted to see what it was that made Barclay Augustus Chesterfield tick. And now that I have..." I offered Jacques a woeful smile. "I almost wish I hadn't. Almost." I held up a hand.

94

"Because now I understand a little bit more about him than I did before. More than I did twelve hours ago. And that matters so much more than me spending four hours crying myself to sleep last night, wishing I was in his arms instead. "Or yours," I whispered. Shaking my hair back, I fixed him with a hard stare, uncaring if he saw the vulnerability inside me. "Which is why I'd like to go shoot something." I completed my pitch and stared at the wall opposite. A particular pitch in my kit that my mother had helped me put together back in the early days when I wasn't so sure of myself and needed to rely on her inspiration to get me anywhere.

Jacques sighed and shook his head. "Come on then."

It looked like that little starter pitch kit still worked.

"Are we heading to the shooting range?" I plastered on a smile, still aching from not curling up with Barclay like I wanted last night. I wished I could go to him now, but he didn't seem to want company if he had pushed this man away who stood beside me.

And I was back in No-Barclay land again, unsure where I stood at all.

"No."

His answer wiped my not so hidden smile off my face.

"No?"

"No." I heard the satisfaction in his voice without looking at him. "If you want to fight, Miss Lockwood, then I suggest we begin a little closer to home."

I snorted. "Are you going to start me off with bows and arrows?" Because that would be so much safer. I'd likely shoot the arrogant preening valet in the tush. Somehow, explaining that little endeavor to Barclay would be both an amusing and horrifying tale.

Jacques smiled slowly. "I'm going to teach you how to use a sword, Miss Lockwood."

I blinked at him. "I don't remember giving you my surname."

His smile widened. "You didn't."

That was twice I'd been blindsided recently, by people who shouldn't have had the information that they did. Casting that information aside for a moment, I focussed on what he just said.

"You want to let me loose in front of you with a pointy object? Are you actually insane?"

"What is it that you Americans say at times like this? He reached a small door just inside the exit to the rear of the house and unlocked it with a key from his pocket. "Jury's out?"

I smiled at his back as I took the epee from him that he passed back, noting the weapon's blunted tip. "Can I tell you a secret, Jacques?" I murmured, taking a step back and raising the sword that felt natural in my hand, its weight an old friend.

"Of course, Miss Lockwood," he murmured, all manners and etiquette.

The tip of my epee pressed to the middle of his spine below his collar. "I'm not American. Didn't my file mention that when you dug me up?"

He stiffened and turned when I let him, sliding his keys into his pocket, his own weapon loose at his side. Loose but not uncomfortable.

For the first time, interest flared behind those gray eyes.

"No, Miss Lockwood. It did not. Would you like to fight?"

I grinned, my anxiety of this morning thrown off within seconds. "Very much, Jacques."

The tall valet led the way out of the house and onto a perfectly manicured lawn beyond the house. I half expected there to be a putting green at one end with a little red flag coming out of a hole.

"It's very you. Wait, do you also cut grass?" I let the innuendo stand.

If I hadn't known better, I would have thought he rolled his eyes.

"Tips on or off?" Jacques rolled his neck. Something popped.

"You shouldn't really do that," I objected. "It's bad for your joints to go all the way around."

"Didn't you just tell me that you were born French, not American? You're very nosy for a Parisian born girl." He laced the words in English, horribly accented as though he strove to make them sound more... Like home.

Because I hadn't called France home in a very long time.

"Tips off," I decided, not having wanted to make that choice at all, but his attitude bothered me beyond any ire I'd felt this trip already and that included having to deal with Barclay's stepmother touching me.

I already understood why he didn't like her, though it wasn't clear exactly why she'd called him back to France, or why he felt the desire to heed her call when he was clearly the one meant to be in charge of his own destiny, but wasn't.

Pacing in a small circle across the lawn, I swept

my blade in a tight arc, rotating my wrist. Something squeezed in my lower back and I regretted not taking the moment prior to warm up while I bitched Jacques out.

Not that the taller man gave me the opportunity before his own blade cut the air and landed a swift point on my shoulder.

The fabric of my lime and green silk top—courtesy of my mother's line from last year—bore a distinct hole. I forced a smile.

"Are you so cheap?" I murmured as we reset for the next point.

A moment later I wished I'd held my peace when he slashed a hole in the other shoulder. I knew I'd remember Jacques's smug grin forever. "From riches to rags," he whispered, his voice carrying on a faint breeze across the lawn as he took two respectful steps back to let me catch the breath I'd barely expelled.

His own exertion barely registered as I raised my blade. Determination set my lips in a fiery smile. "Born with a silver spoon versus earning it, is that right?" I asked softly, my eyes hard.

Jacques frowned at me. "Were you not—"

I didn't let him finish, lunging forward in a double step that he didn't seem to expect after my passive front from before. Caught off guard, he barely raised his blade in time, but by then it was too late. I slipped inside his reach and pressed the tip of my epee to the curve of his neck like a lover's breath, backing off before he blinked.

Jacques raised his hand to his neck, a bemused look on his face as his fingers came away stained with a fine trail of blood.

"Ah, *magnifique*," cried someone behind me.

A smattering of applause surrounded us as I pivoted on my heel. I was unable to school my expression as I took in the small crowd of still hungover guests who had turned out to watch our impromptu display. Staff served mimosas and blinis that they apparently knocked out in time for a festive revival.

I curtsied cutely to a secondary round of applause as Jacques liberated my sword.

"We will settle this in the bedroom," he muttered in my ear, his discontent at being watched without his permission evident.

Mine too, but his sour attitude topped off my morning.

A clock in the house struck the hour twice.

Ah, afternoon. That was fine. But maybe I could find Barclay, after I had cleaned up, and work out just what I could do to help him with his mother's social situation. After all, I was clearly on a roll today. After besting Jacques, nothing could be tougher, surely.

And besides, I missed my fake date that turned out not to be half as fake as either of us expected.

Or not.

CHAPTER NINE

BARCLAY

I didn't see Genie during the day. Jacques, either. My clothes were laid out on the bed as I'd expect of Jacques's perfect service even after my rudeness from before. The only company I had while I ate was from Monique who was clearly in a mood. Maids skittered around her in a flurry to finish their work while she belted out insults willy-nilly. I didn't blame them for their scurrying in the least.

Whispers abounded about a fight between guests. I was far from immune to a little castle—I beg your pardon, chateau, I was in the wrong country in my head yet again—gossip. After I finished my toasted salmon baguette I requested for dinner, I rose and nodded to the man who collected my plates, speaking in an undertone. "Thank you. I am sorry. *She* won't be here much longer. You may share that with the staff."

I didn't care if the rumor got back to Monique or not. Last night and this morning gave me time to clear my head, and rational thought took over once my little tanty time alone in the labyrinth passed. Monique didn't belong in the house. Having it empty was preferable to the bitch who commanded my staff like they were less than stray dogs.

The man nodded at me. His brow dipped. "Monsieur le Marquis," he murmured, his form of the correct address that both Jacques and Genie ignored —one out of playtime and one of ignorance, not that I cared. "Your guests..."

"Ah. I did wonder when this would come up. Please. Enlighten me."

"They fought." He fidgeted on the spot.

I raised an eyebrow. "Did she...slap him?"

The man shook his head.

My lips twitched. "Did he slap *her*?" I'd have words with Jacques if that was the case. He'd apologize profusely, on his knees with his head between her legs for the next month, even if I had to haul his ass back to the States for him to complete his task in person.

Another shake of his head.

I sighed. "Please continue to enlighten me..." I searched my memory for the man's name and came up blank. *Damnit, Jacques was right.* I'd been away for far too long.

"They fought with..." He winced. I waited. He took a breath. "Swords, M- Monsieur le Marquis," he stammered out.

Both of my eyebrows shot for the fresco above my head. "Swords?" A smile tugged at my lips. *What in the hell did Jacques put her up to?* "And did they draw blood?"

"Y- yes, Marquis—"

"What?" I frowned at him. "Who?"

"M-Madame Lockwood, Monsieur le Marquis."

I closed my eyes, tired of all the titles and guff, even as a huff left me. "Of course, she did." I had wondered when the French in her would surface. We played the game, let her be who she wanted to be. Interesting that she chose that moment and that opponent to let her hand show.

And who she fought with on those grounds.

The threat she saw to her happiness. And mine.

I swallowed hard.

"I'm getting rid of that fucking title," I murmured to the air in general, uncaring who heard me.

The man's eyes widened as he stumbled backward, pretending not to have heard my ruminations as a good house staff should, mumbling his appreciation for my presence.

I shook my head. "This place is a mausoleum," I growled. "The only people living here are already dead inside." I stalked through the poached salmon-and-cyan room and ran smack into the monster of the house.

"We need to talk about last night," she hissed at me in French.

I tilted my head to one side, taking in her pink and blue dress that matched Genie's colors from the previous day, knowing she wouldn't wear them again. *Always a step behind, never in front.* "You're right."

Surprise took Monique back a step. She recovered, but with little grace. "I'm glad you agree. Why don't we work in the salon?"

In all that salmon paint and blue carpet that edged its way across the entire bottom floor? Last night's dinner flitted about my stomach in protest. "Here will do just fine. I'll be brief, Monique. Your party last night was the perfect example of what this household shouldn't deal with ever again. You are not of noble line, and three weeks of a gold digging based marriage doesn't count in the least. If my English cousins or their family came to visit, you would host them disgracefully. I can't have your lack of breeding and social etiquette besmirch the family line. In fact, I felt sorry for you, when my father first passed. But this trip has been...illuminating. You may stay tonight and leave early tomorrow. At sunrise please, so you don't disturb the staff in full. Your luggage will be searched. If a single item is found in your possession that you did not arrive with, I will have you arrested."

She squawked, but I stopped listening, making my way through the halls in the long way around the mansion before I arrived at my suite. Closing my eyes, I sent up a prayer that I wouldn't be up for the first of two fights tonight. At least these would come with apologies on my behalf.

Monique was unique in our household, but she wouldn't be my problem much longer, or hopefully theirs.

I pushed the door open to find Jacques standing at the foot of my bed, the room meticulous as expected. A burgundy velvet smoking gown was clutched in his hands.

"My lord." There was that veiled sarcasm in his soft voice that sent rivulets of anticipation along my veins. "I hoped your favorite might be appropriate tonight." He held the jacket out, meeting my gaze head on, the only touch of defiance in his entire demeanor.

"I appreciate the gesture. Truly. Perhaps later. For now..." I pursed my lips and shut the door. "I owe my friend an apology."

Jacques paused. He draped the dressing gown over his arm. "Is that what we are, Barclay?" He swallowed hard, running his fingers over the velvet's soft cut-pile. "I hoped–"

"So did I," I answered softly. "I am sorry in all ways, and I fired Monique."

His lips quirked. "I heard."

"Already?" I wiggled my eyebrows. "My, you are starved for gossip."

This place has been bored and there is nothing worse in France than a bored household. I have neglected them for too long.

I am sorry.

"Masterfully done, sir."

"It was fun," I acknowledged, taking a step forward. "But I shouldn't have taken out my anger on you."

"Or Miss Lockwood."

"Or Genie," I agreed. "I hear you have seen her today?"

He nodded. "She walked in the garden for some time after she bested me."

I laughed softly. "It's been a long time since someone took on a responsibility for me like that. But then, I do have a tendency to drive others away." I thought of Elisse, my ex, and shuddered. Maybe not all of those breaks were my fault, but that woman was in a league of her own.

"Perhaps you should allow others to give you love, Barclay, and not hold us all at arm's length," he reproved me gently.

I winced. "Figured I earned that, huh?"

His lips twisted. "You have become more American than ever."

"Is that such a bad thing?" I raised an eyebrow.

"Why don't we find out?" He placed the gown on the back of a chair and held out his hands. "Let me help you."

I smirked. "Have you been thinking that up all damn day, Jacques?"

"And so English."

"You always liked that part," I whispered.

He said nothing more as he reached out and

tugged my jacket from my shoulders, setting it aside with the velvet gown. A quick flick of his fingers motioned me to hold out a wrist. Jacques turned undoing my cufflinks into an art form. Cool fingers brushed my skin as he worked in utter silence.

"I have been thinking of many things all day concerning you, my lord. How I'd like to wrap your sash around your throat and—"

"My, you are a kinky one," I interrupted his seduction attempt.

"—and throttle you with it." He stared me straight in the face, gray eyes of flint and mouth set hard.

I laughed softly. Lifting a hand to cup his cheek, I stroked my thumb across his jawline, loving the scratch of his stubble against my palm. "I understand the urge."

"Do you?"

His gaze travelled to my mouth where it lingered for attention until my skin began to tingle. Then there was no air to be had in the bedroom, only a tangle of lips and tongues and teeth clashing together with an eternal sense of urgency as he leaned in to devour me. What should have been gentle and exploratory to start fast devolved into frantic, brutal kisses as he backed me toward the bed.

I reached up and grabbed handfuls of his hair, tugging hard. Jacques had always kept the strands long. After I left he seemed to have grown the pale lengths longer than ever. Monique hadn't noticed, but I took full advantage. He growled into my mouth, his hands clutching at my biceps, hard fingers digging in painfully. Lust shot to my cock, leaving me hard and angry.

"It's been too long since I fucked you," I snarled in English, driving my tongue into his mouth.

Jacques broke back for a gasp of charged air, his eyes flaring wide. "I don't remember you ever—"

"Did you think I'd fall on the bed and let you have me, dictate only your terms, my friend?" I snapped, twisting my fingers in his hair as I pulled at his scalp.

The noise that emanated from his mouth was feral as he bowed to my need. "I was looking forward to fucking you," he hissed in a low voice.

Those strands formed the perfect handle. I pulled the slightly taller man's head back until he arched before me. He rocked on his heels, seeking purchase, but I held him in place, unyielding as I stared down at him.

"Then you'll have to wait a little while longer." I smiled. "Because tonight I'm going to fuck you." I spat into his open mouth, watching as he worked his throat and imagined sliding my cock inside it. My smile became cruel. "How many nights were you kept awake thinking of fucking me, and now it's for your holes I'll use instead?"

I didn't give him a chance to answer, pushing him back onto the bed. Jacques stumbled, his knees collapsing beneath him until he lay there, stunned. My name fell from his lips with a delectable sigh as I tapped his legs apart and was on him in a second, rubbing our fully clothed bodies together in a mounting frenzy.

Jacques held my nape tight, keeping our mouths fused together. "The door isn't locked."

I growled and slammed his head back against the bed, furious he'd interrupt my progress. "Let it be unlocked. I'll protect you. "

Shock crossed his features as he stared at me. "But... That's not your job," he stammered.

I shoved myself away from the bed. "I've been doing a shit job if that's what you think." I stepped back, shucking my shirt off and tossed it somewhere behind me. Then I stilled, and watched him.

Wordlessly, Jacques rolled onto his knees and ran his hands over my body. Every plane of muscle reacted to the memory of his touch in tiny shocks.

"I've missed you," he breathed.

My eyes narrowed. "Have you? I always thought you'd move on when I didn't come back," I taunted, enjoying the sense of power overflowing my veins as he knelt for me.

"I hoped," he whispered.

At that I fell silent, letting him explore. Jacques touched my skin as much as possible, exploring with a sense of fragility I wasn't used to from him. He rubbed his body against mine as he pushed my pants open and ran his fingers across my stomach, over the ridges of lean musculature there. When he reached my waistband, he rose unsteadily, circling my body until his chest pressed my back, hard cock against my ass.

Jacques reached around for the buttons on my slacks, his lips pressed to my throat beneath my ear. The soft sounds of sex filled the room as he licked and sucked at my skin.

"No marks," I breathed, flexing my fingers gently at my sides, desperate to drive myself into his body. To reclaim him as mine.

"What if it was your American girl, hmm? Do you remember her touch like this?" He laughed softly. The power shifted back to him as he slid his hand into my boxers, fondling my pulsing cock. His thumb glided smoothly over my head, glossing it with a bead of precum that dripped there. "You always liked silky material." He pushed my slacks away until they pooled around my ankles. "I remember you liked how it felt I played with you."

"I was supposed to be fucking you," I managed.

Hot breath stroked my cock as he extracted his hand to fondle my balls with his fingertips over the silky material that heightened every intimate caress. I shuddered against his body, spreading my legs for him. Air left me as he found my cock again and rubbed me. His other arm wrapped around my waist to press flat on my stomach, pulling me back into him.

"Can I make you come, my lord?" He grazed his stubble along my cheek, pressing a kiss to my temple.

The door swung open. Genie entered, already chattering though I hadn't seen her all day. "That maid, the one your stepmother sent me, is abysmal. Is she an intelligence agent for–"

She froze as she spotted us, her mouth open in a pretty 'o' shape, her eyes taking in everything laid out before her in a cornucopia of sinful evidence. My face heated, lips hanging open as I panted for another lover. Jacques's arm tightened around my waist, his broad hand palming my cock still, stroking gently.

Fuck, if she keeps watching me with shocked eyes like that I think I'll burst.

The concept of spilling myself in Jacques's knowing hand for him while she watched left my cheeks blazing with humiliation. A groan worked its way free of my throat without my permission as I rubbed my ass against his cock.

And Genie never. Stopped. Watching. Us.

A few quick steps brought her back to the door. Her hand landed on the handle, soft lips still parted.

"Genie," I panted, trying to focus on anything other than the erotic rhythm Jacques's handmade, stroking my cock oh so slowly. "I didn't mean for you to see–"

Genie's eyes dropped to my boxers where Jacques put on a show for her, squeezing my swelling length torturously, the head extending past the waistband of my pants. Precum coated my skin, both cooling and embarrassing. Fuck, if he kept this up I'd disgrace myself in seconds on my belly, right before the girl I wanted so badly. Not that she was likely to want to play now. I opened my mouth to object, to lie —*anything*—but she beat me to it.

"For me to miss out on all the fun?" Both

eyebrows rose as she flicked the lock behind her and tested the handle.

Fuck me, I wouldn't last ten seconds between them.

"Want to watch, *chérie?*" Jacques licked a long line along my throat as I moaned for him.

Precum dangled in a long strand from his thumb when he pulled his hand away, leaving me humping the air, desperate and in need. Jacques ignored me. His attention was on another form of prey.

Color flushed Genie's cheeks as she leaned against the wall, running her fingers between her breasts. Her other hand dropped to the short hem of her dress and hiked it up a little to expose her creamy thighs and silky stocking tops.

Jacques' smile grew wicked and positively sinful. "Don't stop playing on our account."

A growl rumbled against my throat as Jacques tilted my head back and kissed me deeply. His fingers closed around my balls, working them slowly, stroking me butterfly soft. "Don't you fucking come, *my lord.*"

"This wasn't what I had in mind." I managed. I couldn't keep my eyes off Genie, flashing her white silky panties, and nearly blew in Jacques's hand despite his order.

Or maybe because of it.

"Change of plans." He gripped my hair and pulled tight, a role reversal of our playtime from before. "You can fuck me some other time, Barclay." He stressed my name mockingly. "Tonight, you can fuck both of us together."

The image of being penetrated by him and sinking balls deep in Genie all at once filled my mind with a delectable image that left me a hot, moaning mess in his arms.

Jacques laughed, the sound low and sinful as he crook his finger at Genie. "Come here, American girl. Allow a true Frenchman to show you a good time, yes?" He wielded the borrowed Americanism like a cracking whip.

She stared between us, her fingers dropping from her scrunched hemline. Genie moved away from the safety of the wall, her steps dainty and unsure to start. Seconds later her hands pressed to my chest as she rose up onto her toes and settled her mouth against mine.

Soft kisses feathered my lips, gentle and tentative. Her gaze broke from mine as she glanced over my shoulder, seeking *his* permission. Something shattered inside me as Jacques laughed again. I kissed her hungrily, winding my fingers through her hair to secure her against me. "Mine. Both of you are fucking mine," I groused, letting Jacques take my weight as I balanced against him to wrap an ankle around his calf.

Genie sighed, sinking her smaller form against me. She mumbled something incoherent against my lips, rubbing her body to mine as I softened my torturous, possessive hold in her hair, tugging gently at the roots until the kiss broke.

Jacques pushed me aside, reaching for her.

"Share," I managed to murmur again.

Her gasp left me aching and straining against the hand that never let me go. His grip remained firm, his touch far too sweet for the situation as his hand slammed over mine on the back of her head and crushed his mouth to hers. Her body rubbed against mine as she responded to his kisses. Soft moans falling from her lips as he worked her like an instrument made just for him. I should have been jealous, but the movement of their bodies with me pinned between them paired with Jacques's ever moving hand on my cock drove me slowly insane.

"Jacques," I gasped, arching as he fisted my cock hard, squeezing until I thought I might burst, though in reality his tight grip prevented me from busting all over her pretty skirt and disgracing myself until I could control my urges.

"Let me," Genie said when Jacques released her.

She slipped her fingers through the tiny pearl buttons on front of her dress until she wiggled her arms out to leave her body bare from the waist up. Then she knelt before me, nuzzling Jacques's knuckles. Hazel eyes raised to him, seeking his permission before she touched me.

He started down at her for a moment, his hand stilling. Then he nodded, leaning down to lick my shoulder and sank his teeth into my flesh as I writhed against the pleasure and pain blossoming beneath my skin. Not that I got much of a breather; as his hand released me, her mouth closed around my cockhead.

"Gentle, *chérie*. He's ready to spill precious fluid." Jacques caressed the back of her neck as she took me all the way to the back of her throat in her hot, wet little mouth.

I fumbled behind me, finding Jacques's fly and tugged his cock free in movements that lacked grace but fuck it, with all their hands on me I could barely focus. I tugged hard until he got the message and moved up beside me.

"Both of us, Genie." I coughed the words out on

a single breath before my throat closed with an excess of pleasure.

Then I couldn't speak at all.

She smiled up at me with eyes aglow with need, curling her fingers around Jacques's cock. Her tongue peeked out between red glossed lips, licking first his cock, and then mine. She swapped between us for a few moments while he caught my mouth again, his kiss searing and brutal, her kisses and licks below sweet and soft. Her moans as I flexed in her mouth drew me back to her, and I broke his kiss unwillingly.

"I don't know I can do this and still fuck you both," I whispered, any shame at needing them both long gone. All I wanted was to give back the pleasure they gave me, and I couldn't do that if I came too fast.

"Then you'll have to hold on." Genie rose and shimmied out of the rest of her dress, sliding her panties down her thighs as we both watched, leaving her in her garter and stocking top. We fondled each other as she got naked and spread her legs, watching us with a question in her eyes as though unsure if she would be the one who would be left out in this equation. "Barclay?" Her head tilted to the side and for the first time, a note of hesitancy entered her voice.

I understood her worry. This was new ground for me, too.

In the past I'd had lovers, shared them with Jacques, too. But that had been an all male event. He knew I'd had women, but he'd stayed away, as I had from him when he'd been encouraged to *entertain* the guests who threw themselves at him. And while I understood he had some bisexual tendencies, they were rare. Jacques was a man's man in all senses. If he wanted her then this was...

Beyond everything I'd experienced with him.

His hand landed in the center of my back as he shoved me down roughly. "Do her well, my lord, or I'll rip you apart from the inside out."

A moan dripped from my lips at the imagery he placed in my head. I stared at the naked pussy laid out before me. Genie glistened before us, and Jacques moved his hand higher.

"Lick."

Grazing my fingertips along her thighs, I found Genie's sopping center and slid two fingers straight inside her heat. She let out a bliss filled cry, tightening immediately and threw her head back at the joy of being filled.

Cold air assailed my balls as Jacques ripped my boxes from me, leaving them around my ankles. My cheeks flushed hotter, knowing he could see me like this, bent over for her and for him. Her moaning, me on the edge. His hand closed tight around my cock in warning, leaving me close to the edge, close to ruin.

Jacques's threat pulsed in my veins until I moaned, leaning down to place my lips over Genie's pussy in a gentle kiss as she shuddered and gushed for me at the lightest touch.

She wasn't the only one to lose it; I moaned as Jacques worked my cock again, finding a condom from my dresser and rolled it on for me as I fingered her. That left me with a narrow timeframe. I worked her faster as he pinched the tip of my cock. The shot of pain doused my immediate threat. I flicked her clit lightly, slamming my fingers home and Genie—

Detonated.

Warmth gushed over my lips. I lapped at her quickly, but barely got to taste her and Jacques took the choice out of my hands, lifting me by my nape and positioning me over her.

"Fuck her, before I take your place if you don't fill her holes," he rasped into my ear.

I knew it wasn't because he wanted to fuck her. Or at least, because he *mostly* didn't want to fuck her. What he wanted was to deprive me of fucking the girl I'd brought to France, take away the prize I'd sought who came to me despite my unusual needs.

"Please," I choked out, knowing I needed his permission to fuck her. "Please, Jacques."

He growled, low and possessive in my ear as he grasped my cock hard and gave me a rough pump. I watched his hands as he guided me into her, working my hips by pulling on my cock. When I nestled into her entrance, her hands gripping my forearms tight and breaths shallow, he pushed hard on my ass with his hips, his cock nestled just between my cheeks, but not inside me, until I sank deep into her. My head hung as I tried to fill my lungs, but the hot, tight sensation of being inside her was almost too much.

As though sensing my impending end, Jacques gripped my hair and ripped my head backward. "Remember my promise." He let me go and slapped my ass, the pain doing precious little to back me off the edge.

Moving with determination, I leaned down to kiss Genie, taking my time to savor her mouth for once, teasing her tongue with mine. She kissed me back breathlessly, stroking my arms and shoulders with increased need as her pussy wept around my rubber encased cock in the worst form of torture.

Fuck it, I needed to feel her walls bare on me,

but I knew I wouldn't last seconds with that perfect pleasure.

Her hips lifted. She met each thrust, urging me deeper with her heels against my thighs until I worked us into a frenzy. It didn't take long with our teasing before she strangled my cock in her tight pussy and let out a small cry. Her breasts flushed the same color as her cheeks, nipples pebbled against my chest as she panted beneath me, her eyes wide as she looked over my shoulder.

"Good boy." Jacques patted my rump as he pulled my cheeks apart.

Something cold drizzled on my ass. My cock jerked inside Genie, earning another moan from her.

"Draw it out," I managed through gritted teeth. "Give her as much pleasure as you can."

"Oh, you'll be the one doing that, my lord." Jacques licked my ear and reached around me. He fondled my balls gently as his cockhead pressed to my asshole, stretching the muscle that hadn't been used for some time. The familiar burn started as soon as he pushed forward. "Someone's been saving himself," he mocked me.

I fought back a groan, my cheeks on fire as I stared down at Genie. His words and tone were designed to drive my humiliation before her to the height of my edge and they did just that.

But she cupped my cheeks in soft hands, her touch tender. I focused on her.

"Show me," she whispered, leaning up to press a sweet kiss on my lips, parting my mouth with her tongue as she explored and tasted me.

I let her, opening to her kiss as her pussy welcomed me deeper. Letting out a moan, I settled between her legs, rocking gently into her cunt as she sighed, moving with me, letting me make love to her.

Jacques growled at the sentiment, pushing forward until he buried himself balls deep in my ass, the glide pure insanity with the silky lubricant that opened me to his abuse. The weight of him pushed me deeper into her, and the dual pain and pleasure massaging both my cock and prostate was too much.

I held to my original promise, pistoning my hips like a madman, reclaiming the power in play and fucking them both.

For a moment I lay there, stiff, a wretched moan drawn out as he ripped into me, and I impaled her. Then I shifted, sliding my hole along his cock, embedding my shaft deeper into Genie's soaked cunt and back again. Over and over, taking and giving at once. My mind splintered with the excess of pleasure. Hands gripped me from all sides, our moans and cries mingling until ultimate pleasure rippled down my spine. Genie fluttered about me too fast, unraveling beneath me but I had no control and couldn't stop. My balls tightened. Jacques slammed into me faster, working himself deeper, harder.

"Hold. Fucking. Out," he grated, sinking his teeth into my other shoulder.

The bite would mark but I'd wear his marks with pride.

The concept was too much. He roared, his cock thrust deep as he came. Heat filled me, dirty and filthy, marking me a second time with a frightening level of violence.

Genie whimpered at the sight of his claiming me as he fucked into us both. I cradled her face, still fucking them both madly, knowing the over sensitivity after coming would be too much for Jacques, but I couldn't stop.

His cock pulsed in my ass, spilling his seed directly into me. Some trickled out, running over my balls in an erotic massage, coating her thighs. My thrusts increased, needing to come before need consumed me. Beneath me, Genie whimpered before she threw her head back on a scream, bearing down and I couldn't hold back.

I came with her, burying myself to the hilt in her sweet, hot depths as she writhed beneath our entwined bodies. Jacques wrapped his arms around all three of us, covering my back and neck with his kisses before he leaned across me and found her mouth, too. Her whimpers became sighs, then I joined them in a tangle of three tongues and lips.

For a time that's all there was. Panting and hot breaths. Unhurried kisses full of whimpers and whispers, the taste of their mouths on mine.

And a promise that tomorrow would be unlike any other sunrise we'd seen.

CHAPTER TEN

BARCLAY

I woke the next morning in a perfect Genie and Jacques sandwich.

"This isn't the worst way to find out that the sun is just rising," I murmured, kissing her deeply then leaned back to offer him my mouth.

Jacques brushed his mouth over mine, kissing me slow and deep, reaching past me to bring Genie closer. "Don't forget your female," he whispered huskily.

"I like him. A lot," Genie murmured in my ear, meeting his eyes over my shoulder. He drew his fingers across her breast, caressing the soft mound to draw a moan from her, then tweaked her nipple until she giggled and batted him away.

His chest rumbled against my back as his hand dropped to the curve of my ass. He fingered my hole gently as I groaned. "Are you sore?"

"A lot," I whispered, squeezing my eyes shut between gasps of pleasure lanced with pain until I couldn't distinguish between them. "It's been a long time since you railed me like that."

"So hot." Genie leaned away a little and fanned herself. "This has been the best sex I've had hands down, but I'm not sure I can go round two right now."

"Me either," I said regretfully, gathering her in my arms and rolled onto my back.

Jacques leaned over both of us, kissing me, then dropping his mouth to claim Genie's in a deep kiss. "Thank you, American girl," he murmured tenderly as he rubbed his cock between my legs.

My heart and cock thrummed at his tone, taking pleasure in seeing my lovers enjoy each other.

"I wouldn't have missed it. And remember..." She tweaked his nose. "*Je suis Français.*"

He laughed low in his throat. "I should have known." A sadness thrummed through him to me. "You leave today. It's been...fun." He shrugged at the lack of romantic expressionism, and drew us all into a bear hug, burying his face in my shoulder still tender from his love bites from last night.

I swallowed hard, glancing between them. "I love you," I said softly, catching Jacques's eye. "You fucking well know I do," I added when he stared at me, unblinking.

"Yes but you know..." He waved his hand over me. "You're a marquis and I'm just a—"

"Bloody good fuck, a fun date and someone I want with me always." I smiled and drew his head down for a kiss. "And Genie. It was meant to be pretend, all of it. But somewhere along the line—"

"Don't you dare," she whispered, her eyes shimmering. "Don't, Barclay. Because if you do, it makes it real. And this, this? It's a fairytale."

"It's our fairytale." Jacques surprised me by speaking up. "And for a French American girl, you fuck very well," he murmured. "But you also look after our lord, and that means everything."

She stared at him, then back at me. "So, we're doing this?" she asked in a quiet, stunned voice.

I smiled, tugging her up my chest and bending an arm around her. "Yeah, Genie. We're doing this. Come back with us." I looked up at Jacques.

He stared back and slowly shook his head. "No?"

"You can't say that," Genie whispered, looking scandalized. "If he asks, you say *yes,* Jacques!"

He laughed softly. "Your stepmother is still here. I heard the car leave earlier, but I think that was the driver...what do you say? 'Abandoning ship'? Who will organize the household, and curb a mutiny in your absence? Who will wait for you until you return?"

I swallowed hard. "I wasn't—"

"You weren't planning on coming back, my lord?" he asked, tipping my chin back and hovering his mouth over mine.

"No," I said, my mouth dry.

His kiss was soft, sweet, then deep and demanding.

"Then, sir, I will give you a reason to come back, and a reason to stay. You too, Genie," he added, curling a finger in her hair. "We will not be complete without you."

I watched his eyes carefully and was blown away at what I saw there. "You love her too."

He froze, then, his eyes still locked on her, gave a slight, jerky nod. "I'm starting to see why you do."

"No," she whispered. "That's not possible." She blinked. "Wait, you said–"

"I did. Now hush for a little while, Genie. I want

to remember this morning, and I don't want to waste a second of it with either of you."

She snuggled into my side. "You're impossible."

"And you're American."

Genie shifted and then suddenly she straddled me, shaking out her mane along her back and wiggling those beautiful breasts. "Then I'll show you all the ways an American *French* girl can play."

I laughed outright as Jacques made a disparaging noise, reaching out to graze his hands reverently over her body. It was the same way he touched me. Despite the distances between time and place I knew then we would be okay and that somehow, some way, we would make what started out as a fake French castle date cum chateau land work.

Because I wasn't letting either of them go. The best part was that I knew neither of them would run from me either. Something in me calmed and for the first time in many years my father's estate once again felt like a home.

And yet, it wasn't.

I closed my eyes, letting my thoughts drift as Genie sank her perfect body over mine, riding me slowly in the morning light. I filled her pretty little pussy even as my cock ached with overuse and abuse. When my balls tingled, I gripped her hips, pulling her down sharply, prepared to fill her, but my thrust didn't go anywhere.

Instead, Jacques's long fingers encircled the base of my dick, his other hand pulling firmly on my balls. The tingle retracted leaving me with a ruined, partial orgasm, a hard cock still inside Genie's hot pussy, and horny as all fuck.

"What the hell was that," I gasped as he glared at me.

"Get your hands above your head," he hissed. One hand tightened on my balls when I didn't immediately comply. "Or I'll make sure I hold on for a while longer."

I gritted my teeth as his hand closed on my balls like a vice. "Yes, Sir," I murmured my appreciation for his craft, keeping the wince off my face and spread my legs submissively. "Is there another way we can serve you?"

He smiled, his face more than a little feral at the role reversal while Genie rocked above me, ignoring our little domestic. "You're going to provide our little Madame here with a perfect platform to come on until she's sated, and you're going to finish the thought you had before. The one you didn't voice," he warned me, leaning on one side. His gaze switched between the two of us as he massaged my balls lightly and squeezed the base of my cock.

I wasn't sure if I had rushing fluids, or no fluids at all.

"Fuck," I managed as Genie rode me slowly. Her body arched and fell, curved thighs trembling as she found the pace that worked for herself. Her fingers dropped between her legs, her head hanging back as she stroked her clit.

Jacques growled low in his throat, leaning forward and spat. She jerked at the intrusion that brought her out of her daydream state and screamed softly when his tongue lashed her clit. He circled her bud as I watched, felt her walls quivering around my granite length.

A hot flush slicked over me as she came. Her hands drifted to trace over her nipples, light touches that left the peaks stiff as Jacques drew back. His mouth was glossy with her cum as he leaned down and licked my lips.

"Leave it," he warned, and my cock jumped inside her to the music of her moans. "Smell like her. Wear her cum. I'll fucking paint you in her scent until you tell me what I need to know."

No honorifics this time. I was pretty sure he

knew what I had in mind. He just needed me to voice it.

"Fuck me sweetly, Genie. That's it, my love," I murmured, leaning back like I had all the time in the world.

Genie nodded happily, fucking my cock with her glistening cunt while my man strangled my balls and threatened their very existence.

He squeezed tighter and I moaned, opening my mouth beneath his, though I knew he wouldn't kiss me. Not with her on my lips, and not because he didn't want to taste her. But because he wanted to torture me with what he wouldn't give me today.

"I want to renounce the title. The house and land can go to someone else. I don't know which cousin it is. Barrogenet will know. He's been my father's *avocat* for many years." I used the French term that rolled silkily off my tongue, trying to concentrate through Jacques's brand of pain. "If there's anything that man doesn't know about his family, I'll be shocked. Monique can leave. I don't care. But also that way the accounts, the house and land...it will flourish under someone else." I shrugged. I had more than enough to provide for myself, genie...Jacques, if he wanted it. To come with me. My heart leapt at the concept.

"Or not." Jacques murmured, watching me carefully. His grip loosened slightly.

I nodded, letting out the breath I'd been holding and not because of how he touched me or how she fucked over us to her own music. "Or not."

That was my main concern. That the staff I'd brought back on would be lost. Left. Abandoned, as I had left them before. Because he was right, again. When I left this time I wasn't coming back. There was no chance at all.

The house and the land...I'd been out of place here since the day I was born. Tried to fit in. failed. Tried to find friends. Family. Love.

Failed at all of those.

At least, I thought I had. It's why I walked away in the first place. Now, I wondered if I hadn't been wrong after all.

"I'm sorry I stayed away for so long," I whispered, stroking Jacques's cheek. His face shimmered as he brushed the wetness from my cheeks.

"It took you long enough." His kiss melded Genie's taste that mixed with his own across my lips. Light fingers squeezed my balls. "Are you sure, Barclay? This cannot be undone. Any of it." His next kiss stunned me to silence, filled with the sort of sweet tenderness that didn't come from sex or lust or loss.

But real love.

From the heart.

"Yes," I gasped, nestling closer to his side. "I'm sure. I want to let go of this place. Come back with me. Come back to the US. But first," I forestalled his argument. "You have to remember, this isn't my only *other home.*"

Recognition flashed across his overcast gaze. "What did you have in mind?"

"I need to go to England."

"I have to attend a gala." Genie grimaced and gasped, leaning forward to scrape her nails across my chest. "Tonight. Fuck, I forgot. In Lon- London." Her breath hitched. "I booked tickets."

I shrugged, pretending her fluttering pussy didn't nearly end my world right then and there. "Unbook them. I have a plane."

She nodded, already fading out of the conversation as her hips rolled and her rhythm resumed.

Jacques watched me. "You understand this is real, Barclay. It can't be undone."

I clasped Genie's luscious as fuck thighs, and nestled deeper into the mattress. "Don't let go of my balls for a bit? I want to watch her come a while longer."

"It'll ache like fuck afterward," he warned me, his brow dipped, and I knew this conversation wasn't over just yet.

Genie stared down at us, rolling her hips as she panted softly. Heat surrounded my cock as she came beautifully for me on demand, her cum sliding around my cock and Jacques's hand to glaze my balls.

Maybe I could beg him to lick them clean. *After*.

"Yeah, but it'll be worth it."

CHAPTER ELEVEN

BARCLAY

I stared at the collection of shoes that overpopulated the doorstep of Bracksley Castle like it was any other uninhabited home. The flight across France in my own jet was faster than even I expected, and a single phone call was all it took to access Barrogenet's office. Apparently the man didn't have a home, and slept and worked in his office, even on a Sunday.

Now all we had to do was get Genie to her gala in London, and our weekend away would be complete.

Though part of me wanted to stall in England for a while longer and figure out what on earth was going on with this place. Apparently I'd abandoned it as much as I had my French obligations. While the stepmonster looked after La Borde, this place was completely abandoned.

Apart from the excess of cheap flip flops.

"At least Killman is doing his job." I poked at a flip flop with the toe of my loafers gingerly.

Jacques kicked the footwear away like it had personally offended him by touching me. "I don't think this qualifies as *'doing his job'*," he snarked, his French accent thick in the pervasive English air, already cool for the season.

I hoped Genie had brought winter evening wear with her, though there was sure to be something vintage in the upstairs rooms, as long as the moths hadn't gotten to the wardrobes.

His curled upper lip hadn't touched his teeth since we landed. Genie was right. Jacques was a snob. But I valued my life too much to be the one to tell him that. Besides, I found his sense of entitlement rather... Charming.

"You have a caretaker called Killman?" Genie pressed tight to my side, glancing around the overgrown acres of gardens, the statues poking out like so many fairytalesque features. "Is he... Safe?"

"Imagining a wild man, my love?" I stroked her

hair with light fingers, suppressing the need to strip off my clothes and run naked through the overgrown gardens of Bracksley.

Mind, not that there was any but the two lovers at my side to see me frolic. Even then it wouldn't be that far outside my usual occupation. Still...I pressed a kiss to the top of her head.

"Killman is our groundskeeper."

"He's doing a fabulous job." Jacques managed to keep his voice free of all accent, and put on that horrible Americanism.

"Are you jealous of his freedom?" Genie murmured, poking her head around my arm at him.

I didn't need to look at her to know she had that glint in her eye that spoke of trouble between them. But I also knew she'd pegged him.

Speaking of, I owed the man a damned good fucking after the way he turned the tables on me the night before. Not that I'd be able to perform any time soon. Not after the way he'd had my balls in a literal vice grip for nearly an hour, or so it seemed while we watched Genie dance for us on my cock at sunrise before we left the chateau.

And every second of my pain had been worth it to be close to them both.

"Why don't we go inside?" I suggested, gesturing to the door. "Perhaps Killman set the fire inside."

Jacques snorted, and Genie shivered on command.

And as expected, they were right, and I was wrong.

The interior of Bracksley Castle was as warm as the weather outside.

"Okay, so maybe Killman needs a little help," I said slowly, looking around at the pile of multimillion dollar stones that comprised my English seat. *Marquess of Bracksley.* There were other parts to it, but that was the important bit. My lips rolled inward. "Perhaps a lot of help?" I hedged.

It didn't look like anyone had been inside the castle since my father passed. I had not returned to England then, bypassing the trip in my haste to escape everything and head to the US and my freedom. My future.

Right now, that selfishness looked like a truly horrendous idea. At least Monique hadn't gotten her fangs into this place. Barrogenet and his British counterpart, Lansdowne, had Bracksley wrapped up so tightly that I didn't think it was even on her radar. But that left the rest of my copious questions begging and unanswered.

Had Killman let the staff go? Or just scared them out of their wits, perhaps. I rolled my neck, relieved when Jacques's hands pressed against my pressure points in a sensual massage.

"You know it was your stepmother," he murmured, his words lacing intrinsically with his actions. "Somehow she found out about this place, and linked it to La Borde. And somehow, she's managed to cut off their income. It won't take me more than a morning's work to head into the village and find out when it happened, fix the contracts and get the staff back, or hire new workers. Give me a number, and I'll see it's done."

His skills were legendary, already running dual duties at La Borde. But this....

"Did you upskill while I was away?"

"I foresaw a need." He didn't look at me, walking further into the room before he turned on his heel to face me. "And I hoped you would return."

All that on a simple hope.

I stared at the empty fireplace and made my decision. "The land is three quarters the size of La Borde. Stables double. I have no idea what's still there. Have a quick gander before you walk into town, please. I'm sorry if there's no car. Ride, if you want. There might be bikes in the garage. Actually, there should be cars, unless someone filched them all. My father has—or had—a collection of Aston Martins. See what happened to those?" Desperation clung to me that fast became an anxiety attack.

I didn't give a shit about the money. My father fucking loved those cars. Almost as much as he loved my mother. I'd be devastated if they'd be stolen or sold out from under us, even after his death.

Genie wrapped her arms around my waist, snuggling deeper. I wrapped my arms around her in return, but when she looked up, it wasn't at me. Her plea went out to the man who stood before us.

"I'll see it's done, my lord." Jacques feathered a reassuring kiss behind my ear as he passed us, taking the scant information in his stride.

No doubt he'd look around before he took off for the village. I trusted him. I had to. Trust required giving and he had given me so much. My stomach revolted on my, and I grasped about and found—

Genie.

"Will you show me upstairs?" she murmured, waving a hand toward a banister and circular staircase that led upward.

I missed the tip of her nose. "I think I love you," I whispered as her eyes widened.

And I meant it.

* * *

Watching Genie flit from room to room in full discovery mode in the eastern wing was a singular joy I couldn't have foreseen. I'd managed to tow my armor in its case up the stairs with me. It marked the carpet somewhat, but it was finally where it belonged—in its proper home.

And now that I no longer had to follow the demands of my cold roast leftovers of a family dinner, I had the opportunity to take pure pleasure in just watching her and that was possibly the best part of my day.

"What time is this thing with your mother tonight?" I ran my fingers across the top of a white sheeted piece of furniture. I thought this was a sitting room, but I wasn't entirely sure. It had been years since I came into this wing. "And do you have clothes?"

"Clothes, yes. It starts at ten, so I can arrive at eleven and probably pull off a red carpet worthy entrance. Midnight would upset her beautifully. Can I borrow a car?" She looked over her shoulder at me and managed to toss her hair all in one flick.

"Are you drinking? Because I'll get us a driver."

My lips twitched at the memory of the last time I had her in a car.

Or when I didn't have her, more to the point.

Genie frowned. "I know we just did non-battle with your family, Barclay, but really, I don't want you to have to deal with mine. *Caustic* is a sweet term if you want to look at it that way. She'll shred you and... I don't want you to be hurt." Her frown deepened.

I instantly hated the way her eyes saddened. Pushing away from my post at the doorway where I'd settled after attempting to catalogue the room in my memories and failing obnoxiously short of the required mark, I crossed the parquet floor and stood before her.

"Genie, you've battled my ex-lover, put up with my stepmonster and flown a quarter of the way around the world just to be my fake date." I tucked a wayward strand of blonde hair behind her ear.

"Your *not* so fake date," she corrected me. Her smile left me less anxious than I'd been a moment before, but still the fact that I'd be leaving her with a foe of her own tonight bothered me.

"Alright then, a not fake date," I conceded, dropping a sweet kiss against her lips and pulled away before she could object. "This morning I suffered pain just to watch you dance over my cock. And I'd do it again because that image of you is burned into my mind, *mon petit chou.* She bit her lip when I held up my hand to forestall her further objections. "Either way, I don't want you heading out alone. One of us should be with you at all times."

Genie stamped her foot. "You're not my keeper, Barclay,' she said, a dangerous glitter in her kitten eyes.

I leaned forward. "And you're far too tempting. Someone will snatch you away from me and I'll raze this city to the fucking ground just to claim you back.

That little declaration against her independence stifled her remaining breath.

I stood back satisfied, until a cold pressure against the back of my head stilled me in a different way. A secondary sound, a muted *snick* told me I hadn't misread the situation.

Or rather, I had, and the danger I spoke of wasn't out there at all.

It was in here with the two of us.

"I'd listen to him, if I were you. In these large cities, you never know who is about and might take a liking to a, what was the term you used? Something *tempting* like you?" Beau Bennett shifted into the room.

I ground my teeth hard enough for the sound to

be audible. "What the fuck are you doing in my house?"

I could almost hear his eyebrows soar for the floral motif decorated ceiling. This one had fleur de lys incorporated into the design to show the marriage to the French side of the family at some point several hundred years back.

"I've been trying very hard to find you, Barclay. First France, now here. You do get around, don't you? Or rather, your armor does." He clucked his tongue at me and the pressure at the base of my skull eased as Beau tucked the gun away.

I closed my eyes, willing blood to flow back to my brain as the answer hit me. "You air tagged my fucking luggage."

Beau laughed. "I air tagged your family heirloom," he corrected me. I suspected you'd need it, or that it would lead me to an answer I needed. In any case I was both right and wrong. And here we are." He nodded jovially and reached out to Genie. "Darling. I haven't seen you for an age."

She weathered the kiss he placed on her cheek with pinked skin and closed eyes.

When those hazel eyes fluttered open, her gaze pierced my soul. "We used to date," she whispered, staring at the floor.

"I get it," I stage whispered back at her from behind my hand. "I used to have a crush on him until I realized that all the pretty faces in the world didn't matter if there was nothing there in either the heart *or* the brain department."

Beau growled and Genie giggled.

I didn't give a fuck about his reaction, but I did damn well care about hers. Holding out my arms I moved sideways, away from him. If he was here to kill me about the damn armor, then he could get it over with. I was too tired to fight today. But he wouldn't do it without me being between him and her.

I knew Beau Bennett had plenty of dark tendencies. He simply didn't need to display them in my house.

"I'd disagree—" Beau started, but his spine stiffened. Suddenly I wasn't the only one in the room grinding their teeth.

"I was wondering when you'd get back. How did you go to the village?" I called over Beau's shoulder.

"Fabulously. We have a three quarter contingent of staff on a promissory note bearing your father's dual solicitor's name—is that what it's called here?" Jacques leaned around Beau to catch my eye, his brow furrowed as he pressed the gun tighter to Beau's flesh.

I shrugged. "It's close enough for this conversation. What did you hear?"

"Enough. Is it just you?" Jacques addressed Beau. "Be clear, please." His accent dropped and I wondered what other upskilling my lover had done in recent years.

Genie stumbled back into my arms. "What's happening?"

I placed two fingers over her lips. Explanations could come in a moment.

"Just. Me," Beau seethed.

I nodded to Jacques. "Truth. He's angry because he didn't know."

Jacques smiled and nudged Beau further into the room. "As it should be."

Genie turned in my arms. "What didn't he know?"

I smiled down at her. "Jacques's first duty is as my bodyguard. He has been since I turned seventeen, though his duties as my valet began when I was eighteen. The year we became lovers." Friendship blossomed. Jacques, then nineteen and a few scant years older than me, took the time to teach me the skills to defend myself as his first ever client.

But that was where his duties stopped, geographically speaking. He never travelled with me to keep that cover in place. Because France was where the money lay. Here in England, there was less threat, or so my father assumed. It looked as though I had brought my own problems with me from the States.

My reminiscence could wait, however.

I stared at Beau, gathering Genie in my arms and motioned for Jacques to step back after our insurgent handed over his weapon and two blades that were found on him. "Why are you here? You didn't track me across the globe for my silver collection."

Beau snorted. "I'm here for her."

Both Jacques and I stiffened.

"Never going to happen," he murmured, raising the gun a second time.

Beau smiled faintly. "Interesting. I thought you only batted for Team Barclay."

I swore Jacques actually growled.

"However," Beau continued, as though he was never interrupted at all, "I'm here for one person, and it's neither of you boys."

My arms tightened around Genie. "What?"

"I said no, Beau," Genie sighed, leaning her head on my chest like she'd been through this conversation before. "And don't you have your own problem child at home?"

I snorted a laugh at that. I was sure Sylvie would be delighted at being called Beau's *problem child.*

Beau smiled. "She probably calls me hers," he mused. "And I'm flattered, but no. That is... of the past." he flicked a lint from his blazer. "This afternoon's entertainment starts before the main event. Or did you not want to see your mother at the gala dinner, or ever again?"

CHAPTER TWELVE

GENIE

I stood before my mother who wept crocodile tears across a debtor's desk and sighed.

This is why she blindsided me the first time.

Grace Lockwood, my mother, already knew about my trip to Europe before I told her because she had me followed. She already knew, because she was in panic mode. And she was on my case to launch my lines because her business—*hers, not mine*—had failed. Again.

This was not the first time my mother's choices didn't work for her. It simply was another chink in her perfect armor the world never saw. All the lies. The bullshit.

Tonight looked like a last ditch effort to keep it all afloat. Beau Bennett found out about that and for reasons still known only to his own interests, decided to stick his nose where I wasn't sure I wanted it.

So I stood in the debtor's dingy office in a part of London where I'd never been and probably never wanted to be ever again. My mother's hair stood on frazzled ends as she stared at me through lashes clumped together. Her makeup had run and her clothes were torn. The entire building, a warehouse on the edge of Westminster's industrial sector, stank of stale urine.

Mom's skirt was in taters, and she sobbed openly, grasping at my feet as I skittered backward into a hard body. One arm wrapped reassuringly around my waist. I didn't have to glance backward to know it was Jacques.

A pudgy, sweaty looking man leaned across his desk, and leered at me. I half expected a burnt out cigar to hang from his fleshy lips. The whole set up had a noir type feel to it, like something out of a nineties gangster fast talking flick.

Because that's what this whole thing was.

A set up.

Because not only would my mother not only die before her treasured wardrobe was torn or ruined, she didn't have a bruise on her. The whole building and its scents—for the daughter of a luxury brand magnate—was overkill.

And the real tell? Those clumpy lashes and smeared makeup. My mother could be in a multi person porn film as the final event, the money shot mayhem, and her makeup would be *perfect*.

Not a run in sight.

I sighed. "Is this really what you've been reduced to? An act so pathetic you'll wear dime store makeup to con me into whatever it is you're asking for? I said I'd go to the party. You didn't have to pull this charade off to get me to go, Grace." I flicked a hand in Mom's direction. The paid actor on the other side of the desk smirked, and leaned back.

A half smoked cigar emerged from his pocket. He lit the thing, obscuring some of the stale piss that tainted the air. "Told you she wouldn't go for it. I brought in the toy boy, though."

My blood ran cold. "What?"

Beau frowned. "What deal did you make, you pathetic excuse for a maternal unit."

I snorted, and even Jacques laughed, tugging me tighter against his chest. Somewhere in the background, Barclay moved around, exploring. Jacques wouldn't allow him closer to the action than that, and so he was relegated to the distance while we renegotiated my mother's "freedom."

"Don't take her seriously," I scoffed. "Whatever trouble she's gotten herself into, it's not here, Beau."

He turned his frown on me. "Genie, I don't think this is quite the farce you think—"

A soft gasp from behind us broke the pervasive stench that choked us all. I twisted around in Jacques arms in time to see Barclay crumple, but not without taking the shadow behind him to the floor.

Twin flashes lit the space. Both shots were silenced, and all the louder for it.

I stood between the two men with their raised weapons as beau swore softly, striding forward to check on my sobbing mother.

"What do you need?" he asked softly, though his voice had an edge to it.

I suspected this wasn't how he wanted the night to go, but he foresaw the outcome much clearer than I had. I shook my head, ignoring him as I took off at a run, heading for Barclay where he crouched on the floor over the figure all dressed in black.

His white shirt was dotted in the blood of another man. I reached him, the flashlight app on my phone illuminating his face that also bore several dark splattered spots. *Fuck*. He'd freak out if he knew. Barclay was so pedantic about his personal hygiene. I'd seen it in how fastidiously he washed his hands, how often he showered. How disgusted he'd been with himself the night after he spent hours asleep in the garden, passed out drunk.

Tentatively, I raised a hand and slid my thumb nail beneath the largest dot of blood. The man at his feet didn't moan and I doubted he would miss it any time soon. "You're not hurt, are you?" I offered it up as a distraction.

"No," Barclay said softly, watching me with all the patience in the world.

With another careful nail I caught the next drop, and the next, until I almost had them all. His face nearly clean, I admired my work, and him. At least, his demeanor. He didn't shake or break down like I might have expected.

"Your bodyguard does an excellent job," I said softly.

"I know," he whispered back. His voice shook, though I wasn't sure if that was from fear or pride. Maybe a mix of both.

"Maybe you should listen to Beau." Jacques stood tall behind me. I didn't need to look back at him to know that he mirrored Beau Bennett's imposing stature, his unyielding stance.

Perhaps we have our own gangster noir stage after all.

Barclay leaned forward and pressed his lips to mine. "I'm proud of you. Not a single tear. And you never bought into her bullshit."

I shrugged. "Sadly, this isn't the first time she's pulled something like this because her ploy didn't work or she didn't want to sue for bankruptcy. That would be admitting to failure in public. My mother hates letting the world know that her plans have failed." I grimaced. "I stopped falling for that sort of con when I was ten years old."

"A ripe old age to attain wisdom," Barclay intoned solemnly.

"You bet your ass." I kissed him back slowly as Beau snuffed out the still smoking cigar that was as cheap as the rest of the set. I broke away and glanced over my shoulder at him. "How did you know he wasn't a paid actor?" I asked curiously, uncaring that he knew about my own mistake.

Beau paused in the act of grinding the cigar into

ash beneath his patent heel. Barclay wasn't the only one with a penchant for pretty things or a pedantic nature.

"Because he used to work for my father," he said softly, his tone pensive. "I didn't like that he was involved with the mother of someone I used to date."

Someone I cared about.

The unspoken words hung in the air between us.

I swallowed hard, hating that he put me in this placement, but grateful for the heads up all the same. "Th–"

"Genie says thank you." Jacques stepped in front of me, placing his body between Beau and where Barclay and I crouched on the floor. "She says you've paid your debt for any hurt that you may have inflicted on her before, and that you're no longer required here." He folded his hands before himself, including the one holding his gun.

I stared at the back of my newest lover, only able to see his imposing silhouette, crouched on the floor of a dusty, urine scented warehouse, enfolded in the arms of another.

A sort of stillness fell over us all, the city alive everywhere but here.

"I like this shade on you." Barclay broke into the

void, the standoff between dominants above us where I feared to tread.

Breath whooshed from me as I looked down at my blood stained nails, and giggled. "What should we call it? '*Inequity's den at midnight*'?" The name and the whole situation left me giggling harder as Barclay kissed his way down my neck, edging his boot behind the dead man's neck beside us and kicked his body out of the way.

"Call it '*Jacques's Delight*'," Beau said suddenly from the same place where he hadn't moved since ending the life of the cigar smoker opposite my mother. He shot her a hard look. "Shall I take this away and get it ready for your event this evening? It looks as though I'm attending while I'm here on my father's behalf."

I stared, having no idea why Beau Bennett needed to represent the California mafia's don at a London gala charity dinner. But if Beau Bennett said he had work to do, then I wasn't one to fight him on it.

And besides, he was taking a particularly unpleasant job off my hands. Still...

"What will it cost me?" The tightness that had released from my chest a moment before zinged back along my spine. Jacques, with his hypersensitive attention to us, shifted a foot backward. I ran my fingertips along his calf muscle through his pants leg under Beau's watchful gaze.

Fuck it, I'd go down on both my lovers before him just to earn a reaction right now, and I think we both knew it. He might have Sylvie now, but I'd always been a soft spot for him, the girl who wouldn't stay put no matter what he demanded of me. That I'd fallen for two Frenchmen must gall him.

They were both mine and no one else's. Well, except between us, of course. All sharing gratefully permitted.

"I'll take you home, if all this is accounted for?" Jacques caught my elbow at a quick glance to Barclay.

I shook my head. "We're still establishing details." I knew Beau Bennett well. Well enough that his silence spoke louder than any shouted claim. I suspected both men knew as much, but I wanted to understand this debt I'd just walked into. If all I had to do was pay my mother's debt out and dress her for the evening, then I'd manage.

"No," Barclay said firmly. "Let me offer you this gift, my love." he locked eyes with beau over my head, snatching me tight to his chest.

I was halfway through an objection to why that

was a terrible idea when Barclay kissed me. And I realized that of all the times I'd been kissed in my life, that I'd never actually been kissed before at all.

Because Barclay Augustus Chesterfield could *kiss*.

Of the life changing variety.

Soft but firm lips moved over mine, warm and sweet as he encouraged me to open my mouth. I flicked my tongue against his bottom lip, expecting him to dive in, but instead he offered me open mouthed kisses that left me weak kneed and aching as I clung to his ruined shirt, locked safely behind the hard embrace of his arms.

This was the man who demanded his lover take his desire the night before. The same man who I fell for, all twisted and torture, but at the same time fair and kind and so damn cute.

Barclay was all those things wrapped up in a bow tie, a blood stained shirt and perfectly pressed slacks.

When he pulled away, the room stood empty except for us. My mother, Beau Bennett and the bodies were gone, the only evidence of their passing a few blood splotches on the floor and my nails.

Jacques stood in the doorway. His angular, handsome face remained half obscured by shadow as he watched Barclay claim me in a room full of death and lies.

And he never said a word, just watched, his gun at his side, not until we were ready to leave. Then he followed us, shadowing every step. I knew we would be safe until we reached home beneath his gaze.

CHAPTER THIRTEEN

JACQUES

She hated that Barclay offered to pay her debt.

She hated that he didn't come to the gala and chose a quiet night in the castle by himself.

And she hated that I took her out instead.

But I was beyond proud of Barclay—and her—at both of them for how they stood up under the pressure of tonight's bullshit. Neither of them should have been present. I knew neither of them should have gone, but I also couldn't let them stay in the house where they would have been equally as exposed.

I couldn't split myself into two pieces, no matter

how much I wanted to, and I didn't trust the newcomer. With good reason, as Barclay's face told me his position on the man. That was enough for me.

And so we went together.

A good thing as it allowed me to see just how deeply in love Barclay was with Genie...and that he deserved a night off. The threat we discovered was neutralized and it had never been aimed at him, after all. The shadow who had a go at him, it turned out, was a last ditch effort to gain Genie's attention.

Beau Bennett extracted that information from the mother and texted me the information before we made it back to Bracksley Castle. And so I felt comfortable leaving Barclay alone, albeit with an almost full contingent of staff to wait upon him for half an evening without myself or genie in attendance.

The girl draped over my arm caused all the mischief of the night, and now we were going to tidy up a few loose ends before we went home to my lord and his new and thriving household. I'd been pleased to prove myself to him with the small task earlier, show him my worth, that I could provide for both of them in times of need.

And I was comfortable with how I'd left him, with fires running in almost every room, and hot water in his bathtub. I didn't care if I had to bankrupt every hardware store and purchase every axe in the country and hack away at Barclay's overgrown garden or smoke out the castle with green wood. I swore the castle would remain warm.

"How long do we have to stay?" Genie toyed with my cufflinks borrowed from Barclay's traveling collection. The suit had arrived an hour before we departed, tailored to my measurements.

Apparently I wasn't the only one with an eye for sizing up a man's worth.

"Don't you want to find out what tonight was about with your mother?" My own curiosity was piqued. Mostly I needed to ascertain there was no further threat to the girl who had stolen my heart, or at least enough of it to share with Barclay.

The whole situation still sat strangely with me, but he didn't object and so I let their happiness take mine along for the ride, however long it lasted.

She shrugged. Her go to, oh so Americanism when she didn't want to answer me, or so I'd discovered. Genie's personal style was both cute and annoying and evasive all at once.

"I really don't much care," she murmured, staring straight ahead at the red carpet rolled out before us that neither of us had stepped foot onto yet. Her gaze skittered across the plethora of media chattered off to one side with no regard for the hour, and the crowd still yelling at and photographing late arrivals like us who stepped daintily from their limos.

I'd parked the classic silver Aston Martin that Barclay had leant out of the night along the block. We walked in. An unusual entrance, perhaps, but it gave us both a chance to understand the lay of the land. And while Genie's arrival might cause the store amongst the paparazzi prepared to devour their next victim, I was an unknown. I wasn't sure if that would help or hinder her.

As delectable as she appeared in a black sequined dress shot through with silver leaves that reached her knees and sat across the tops of her breasts like a chiffon silk sheath, I wasn't ready to take that chance. She hadn't fallen apart on me yet. That didn't mean she wasn't going to, and I wanted to be there when she did, not shove her in front of the red carpet ravens and watch the drama unfold for Barclay to read about in tomorrow's rags.

He wouldn't thank me for that trauma.

Leaning down, I brushed my lips across the top of her head. *She's so fucking fragile.*

"Shall we discover the service entrance? I've found I'm rather good at locating those." I threw on an English accent that might have been a fraction better than my American one.

Genie winced. "You're an amazing lover and possibly a better bodyguard. But don't quit your day job to become a spy, Jacques."

I chose not to take offense at that remark. "As that lady says. Shall we?"

I held out a hand and directed her down a smallish alley way where I'd spotted black and white uniformed personnel carrying food trays and laundry bags earlier. One was smoking, which left me believing we'd find an extra entrance along this route. Cigarette breaks were hastily stolen and highly coveted, especially in high end hospitality.

Genie let me lead her along the narrow alley without complaint. I smiled at that. Many girls of her status would be sure to raise hell just for being taken out of the limelight. But just like Barclay who needed a few hours to himself, I understood her need to both be here, make an appearance and leave as quickly as possible.

And Barclay was paying Bennett handsomely, I was certain, for the privilege of not detaining Genie any longer this afternoon, or being accosted by her absentee mother.

"Here we are." I sped through a swarm of gape

mouthed staff to find a door hidden behind a cloud of smoke.

Genie ducked beneath my arm, mumbled her thanks to the gawking group, and disappeared into the darkened hallway beyond. I took two steps and found myself face to face with Beau Bennett. He pressed my back against the bricked wall at the side of the hotel that hosted the event.

A thickly muscled chest pressed to mine, arched lips brushing my cheek as he spoke. The other man, around Barclay's age, I assumed, stood as tall as me. Hands gripped my arms hard in warning not to move or make a sound.

I didn't want to fight him, only to not alert the crowd around us until I needed them to know I required their flight or alarm.

Those sensual lips brushed my skin once more. "Tell your girl that her mother isn't worth the effort. She tried to con me twice and steal from me at least once in the space of ten minutes. I'm still counting my pocket change," he murmured ruefully.

"Is that so?" I wasn't surprised as I levered a fraction of a breath's space between us. "Is that all you've discovered?" I kept my voice low and hard. *No freebies from me, college boy.* Neither his wealth, position nor his apparent strength meant anything to me.

The only interesting thing about him was the fact that his body pressed to mine, my cock apparently seized to respond. An action I hated as I kept myself celibate for my lord, and now, Genie. But not only did my body react to his; beau's cock pressed to my hip, hard and thick.

"Aren't you taken?" I said out of turn, surprise lacing my voice.

"Very much so," he whispered back, his voice low and guttural. "Not in my control, I'm afraid."

Suddenly I understood Barclay's fear of the man. Not only did he have power in wealth and status to rival my lord's own, but in a sexual, dominant sense.

"What can you tell me about Grace?" I elected to ignore the man's sexual proclivities in favor of gaining more information on the name I'd heard Genie address her mother with earlier in the night.

"That she is broke. Flat out with not a dime to her name. Count it out in popcorn kernels, pennies or pence. She's skint. And she's pulling in favors from everywhere but she's been doing it for a while so there's not much left. Tonight's con is to get people to give to the charity she runs. A charity which will help people who are in need, financially. Or in this case, just one. She'll take the money and line her own coffers with them. Short of calling the police, there is little we can do. Unless you want to spend the night with your new girlfriend explaining to the London Bobbies why her mother is intent on defrauding the Brit's best and wealthiest this evening."

With that little pre rehearsed speech completed, Beau Bennett let me go and backed down a step.

I watched him, leaning back against the wall and made no indication I was ready to move. "I can see why she wants you."

Beau's eyes darkened. "Genie?" His breath hitched and his hands slid into his pockets too fast.

I let the faintest smile tilt the corners of my lips. "Your little Toy."

Beau Bennet wasn't the only one with a cache of information sources to pull from. Best? I hadn't had to ask either Genie or Barclay. From the pretty share of puce that suffused his cheeks, he damn well knew it.

Genie popped her head out of the staff entrance to the hotel. "Are you coming? Hi, Beau." She gave him a little wave, but her stunning eyes were for me. "I found a fountain. Swim?" Her eyes sparkled with mischief.

The sort I found too addictive to ignore.

I reached for her hand, pulling her out of the

shadows and straight into my chest. "You play, I'll film. It doesn't seem right to leave Barclay at home and not be included now, does it?" I laced my voice with innuendo.

I meant every single word, but I also intended for our conversation to be overheard.

Her infectious giggles left me rock hard. Fuck, I couldn't control myself around her. Was this how Barclay felt all the fucking time?" I didn't look back as I let Genie tow me into the bowels of the hotel. The door shut behind me with only the slightest hesitation, as though someone caught it and stepped in behind us.

But I was too busy chasing Genie along the corridor to notice. At least, that's how I made it look to Beau's green eyed stare as he followed us along the hall at a growing distance.

I photographed Genie with her black and silver dress hitched up around her thighs, splashing in the fountain, half obscured by plastic palms. I took a video of her too, playing and teasing me until she was half drenched. Then I sent both to Barclay.

JACQUES: What you're missing.

BARCLAY: Send me more.

JACQUES: You should be here.

BARCLAY: You sent me to the naughty marquis corner

JACQUES: Aren't you in the bath?

BARCLAY: Maybe?

JACQUES: I expect photo evidence.

BARCLAY: More motivation is required.

I motioned Genie over and cupped a handful of water, splashing it across the front of her dress. Her silent scream, her mouth open wide, hardened me instantly to a point of pain that I savored. I picked a set of open doors upstairs and knew we were never going to make it to the gala.

"Get back in. Barclay wants sexy pics," I murmured, motioning for her to twirl for me as I snapped away, then slid the settings back to video and held up my phone.

Genie danced on demand, running her hands over her body and dropped the straps of her dress.

The material clung to her body with nothing else holding it up. I groaned as she toyed with her nipples, teasing us all as she arched and played.

I cut the video away, sent it to Barclay and pocketed my phone, reaching for her. Genie's hand was in mine before my phone vibrated. I cured in French, ripping the device free.

"It'd better be worth it," I groused, and opened the message to find myself staring at a dick pic.

A dick I recognized, with a sculpted bubble foam heart perched on top, Barclay style.

"Cute," Genie remarked, leaning over my arm as she pulled her heels back unsteadily. She tilted her head to stare up at me with glowing eyes. "I bet you can do better."

I caught her hand and dragged her toward the staircase. "With me, American girl," I growled, towing her after me. She stumbled and righted herself. I knew my stride was too long, but I wanted her to struggle. I needed her to chase me.

Because what came next wouldn't be sweet, and it wouldn't be gentle.

But damn would I enjoy seeing her arch for me when I made her come with my fingers as she watched the crowd from above.

And I didn't care if they saw her, too.

My feet ate the stairs as I took them two and three at a time. Genie's sharp breaths at my back told me she didn't object to my rush. Sharp nails dug into my hand, never pulling away. I gripped her firmly. When I reached the doors I'd eyed off earlier, I gave each a cursory glance and chose the middle room, pulling her inside.

Unoccupied, it featured a glass floor to ceiling window that overlooked the event from above.

The perfect viewpoint for what I needed tonight.

I left the lights off, my arm already around her waist as I yanked Genie forward, almost throwing her full weight against the glass without ever letting go of her wrist. The soft cry that elicited from her sweet lips sent blood hurting to my cock. My shaft strained against my pants, but it wasn't my time yet.

Now, it was hers.

"Jacques—" Her breathy cry transformed into a sigh as I licked along the exposed slope of her throat. "Oh, fuck, that's so good."

"We haven't started yet," I murmured into her skin. "Are you ready?"

"N–no?"

I smiled, and nipped her flesh. "Pull your panties down."

"I'm not wearing any."

My smile sharpened. "Did you do this for my lord?"

She nodded, watching the people milling about below us. "Did you lock the door?"

A laugh escaped me. "No. Be glad I didn't turn the lights on."

The feral little moan that escaped her left me harder than ever. I ground my cock against her ass. "I've never been straight, Miss Lockwood. So why the fuck do I want you so bad? You're like an addiction I can't give up. The hit I want over and over again." I tightened my grip around her waist, inching her dress up until her creamy thighs and bare cunt was exposed to the crowd below. "I want you to watch all those people dressed up and milling about like so many ants. Fucking sheeple following each other. Every one of them deserves to be conned by your mother tonight. Do you know why?"

"No," she breathed, writhing against me, rubbing her ass back on my cock.

I slid my fingers across the front of her bald pussy and found her already smeared with her own juices. "Fuck," I hissed. "You needy little creature." I tapped my fingers gently on her clit. "Open."

Her legs parted. "Is that it, 'the perfect business woman fleeces the masses again'?" She gasped as I circled her clit. From her increased breaths she was seconds from coming for me in front of all of them, and none of them had any idea what we did above them.

"Mmm," I cooed in her ear, sliding my fingers in tight circles over their taut bud. Years in the chateau taught me how to deal with a woman as quickly as possible to get out of their way. Now, I used that knowledge to give Genie as much pleasure as I could, fucking loving the way her knees wobbled as I worshipped her. "Simple, isn't it? And I suspect that both Beau and Barclay will pay her out. This will go on and on unless someone stops her."

"But no one cares," Genie realized. "So she'll keep getting away with it– *ohhhh.*" Her hands splayed on the glass as she came, her legs spreading wider for me as her juices coated her thighs. Genie's body softened and I pressed her against the glass in full.

She came out of her haze, still shaking. "What if it breaks?"

"Then we fall together."

I turned her hard and kissed her as I pressed three fingers deep inside her tight little hole, and laughed into her mouth. "Fuck, you're tighter than Barclay after years without my punishment. You'll be sore tomorrow, little kitten, all stretched out for us."

She moaned for me as I planned, sliding down the wall. I held her up, working my fingers gently inside her. I wanted her on the edge of her arousal, not to rip her apart.

At least, not yet.

Those hands on the glass flexed as I curled my fingers inside her tight walls. "Relax, pretty little kitten," I murmured. "Maybe afterwards I'll let you swallow me down. Once I've destroyed this little pussy. Once you've screamed this place down and they're all watching."

She fluttered madly about my hand. I licked salt from her neck and used my teeth to flick the straps of her damp dress down that she'd pulled back up when we left the fountain downstairs. The semi dry fabric slipped to her waist, baring her breasts. I pressed her fully to the glass, and she gasped. The cold and exposure was too much. Genie creamed my fingers nicely, hot and wet and messy.

I pulled my hand out of her with a sloppy sound that left her moaning, swiping my sticky fingers across her face. "Don't you dare lick that off,' I warned her, tipping her head up to kiss her with tongues only, not erasing her cum from her own face.

She licked my tongue back as I fisted my cock, lubricating myself with her juices. "Please," she murmured into my mouth. "I want to feel you inside me. You and Barclay both—*fuck, Jacques.*"

Her use of my name and a shiver inside her nearly sent me straight over the edge. I swore I'd never had so little control as I had with this girl, and never with a female before. In fact, the only person I'd ever felt like about this was—

"You'll call him *my lord*," I growled, fisting her hair and pressed her face to the glass. She rose onto her tip toes in her sexy little black heels to match the dress ruched around her waist. We'd both be covered in black and silver glitter come morning, but I didn't care. What we were covered in now was the least of my worries. "Whenever you talk about Barclay, you address him the right way." My thrusts punctuated every word, harsh and brutal. Nothing about me tonight was gentle compared to the tease of before.

She tipped her head slightly to one side, the only lenience I gave her. Soft, stuttered breaths heated the glass in a mist that obscured her pretty face. "And what should I call you?"

"Fucking *yours.*"

Her pussy contracted hard. I groaned, pressing my forehead to hers as I railed her. Certain the glass would shatter and send us both tumbling half naked and joined to our deaths on the floor below, I fucked into her harder, faster. She was the obsession I couldn't break. I needed her as badly as I'd needed Barclay over the years. And now I had both of them, there was no way I'd let either of them go.

"Fuck," I panted, sliding one hand down to her hip to run my thumb along the inside of the bone there, finding her sensitive spot. She arched for me as I hit the nerve, clamping down again. After all the teasing, the heat and cream of her and scent permeating our every breath, I couldn't hold my orgasm back.

I came with her, coating her insides with my seed. My roar filled the room, rocking us on our feet. Genie reached back, no longer clinging to the glass as she trembled around me. Her pussy fluttered, legs shaking as she clung to me for support, to hold her up.

Trusted me as no one else but Barclay ever had.

And I—

Couldn't.

My legs shook with the force of my orgasm as I pumped myself inside her. Gripping her tight, I let us slide slowly to the floor in a mess of silk and obsession, and whispered the words I never thought I'd say to a woman in my life.

Certainly not one I'd met a few days before in another country on the arm of another man.

"I love you."

I nuzzled her hair and clutched her tight to my chest, uncaring if she stained my gifted shirt. Because every word was true. The sigh that left my lungs was of the warm and fucking fuzzy variety.

I stroked her hair as I held her in the cradle of my arms, vaguely aware of the shadow that walked away from the doorway I hadn't locked earlier. Probably not my smartest move, but payment for the suit had to come through somehow, and it likely wasn't anything Beau Bennett hadn't seen before. I'd figured he wanted to check in on her before he left, and I expected he liked what he saw. Otherwise I guessed I wouldn't be breathing.

Ignoring his soft words without trying to interpret them, I closed my eyes and held Genie to me tighter. I didn't need someone else's approval.

The girl pressed to my chest was mine and I'd share her with one other man and one only.

EPILOGUE

BARCLAY

I stretched out in a chintz baroque arm chair that I had no idea on the history of, other than that its previous occupant had a tendency to sit with their hips skewed to the right more than the left. My heels rested on an overstuffed, if slightly threadbare footrest that showed plenty of prior love for the piece. A fire burned low as I read from one of my grandfather's leather bound copies of Byron. He'd marked it up in places. Some of the comments were academic based as though he'd made them during his college years. Others were obviously added over the top later on and far more derogatory.

I wonder what you would have thought of me, grandpa.

But I'd never had the chance to meet the man past my fifth birthday. I barely remembered anything beyond a wrinkled visage full of whiskers that scratched my face, a gruff voice that scared the hell out of miniature versions of me, and a man who smelled more than faintly of good tobacco that had been all the rage back then.

Jacques had committed to filling the house with staff and warmed the stones of the old, uninhabited castle before he and Genie left for the night in his shiny new suit that Beau sent over, courtesy of my directions. I hadn't had time to duck into my favorite tailor when we arrived as we were in a bit of a rush to get to Bracksley, but Beau stood up to the task magnificently. I knew it would cost me, but that was life at Rippton U. We traded favors the way others lent out shirts of traded books or other collectibles.

When you had a personal bank account with funds enough to purchase a small country, favors between flirtatious enemies meant more than any other bribery could achieve.

I rolled the yellowed corner of the page as my eyes began to droop. Lines blurred as I shook myself back to some semblance of a waiting state. I'd promised both Genie and Jacques that I'd stay awake and wait up for them, but the exhaustion of the weekend set in. I'd also promised them we'd head back to the US after this, but unlike in France, I didn't have the same urge to depart post haste. Some part of me wanted to steal a few more days in the suddenly warmed castle. Pick out the bones of who I was, who we all were together. Maybe discover a part of my own history here, and explore with them who we wanted to be before we went anywhere together at all.

Steal a few moments of peace before Rippon attempted to shred it apart.

Closing Byron's ancient pages—the book was possibly a first edition, knowing my family—I placed it on the over padded arm of the chair and rested my head back, letting my eyes close. *Just for a moment*, I promised myself, knowing that it would be far more.

And when I opened them—more than a moment later, though it seemed as though no time at all had passed—Genie curled in my arms, her legs tucked over my hips. Curls hung in a disheveled mess over my shoulder and her makeup smeared across her face. No, not her makeup...

I frowned, leaning in to kiss her and came up

with a mouthful of heady scent that left my sleepy brain suddenly hyper alert.

"My, you did have fun without me," I reproved her gently. Teasingly, as I didn't really disapprove.

Neither could I rise to the challenge tonight, too exhausted to play. And she was warm in my arms, her eyes dozy as she snuggled into me. I doubted that, whatever the hell they had done together, that she was in a fair state to play, either.

I glanced over my shoulder and around the chair for Jacques, but the taller man was nowhere to be seen. "Did you not bring him back with you, *mon petit chou?*" I murmured, pressing my mouth to the corner of her lips and tasted her, but not him. My brow gathered. "Did you not please him, my love?"

Surely she wasn't that inconsiderate? Or perhaps he hadn't let her... My mind whirled with the possibilities. Jacques was demanding, and sometimes refused to allow others to pleasure him, preferring to watch as his lover unravelled, refusing to take part at all.

Was that what had happened between them tonight?

"She wore me out is all, my lord." Jacques's equally sleepy voice came from the floor somewhere in the realm of my feet.

I peered over Genie's knees at him. "What on earth are you doing down there?"

"Well, I won't fit in there with all of you, so here I am." He spread his hands as he rested his head against her thigh, stroking beneath the hem of her damp gown thoughtfully.

My frown deepened. "Why are you wet all over, kitten?"

She shrugged. "The fountain looked fun to play in. Then Jacques took me upstairs."

My frown cleared as my eyebrows attended my hairline at her neat use of the double entendre I was sure she intended. "Did you actually go to the event at all?"

"Nope."

"Ah." I let her settle into my for a moment, stroking along her body until my hand met Jacques's. His fingers found mine, tangling together tightly. My heart lurched hard in my chest as he pushed her into my arms harder then pressed his mouth to my knuckles gently.

Not asking forgiveness, or begging for something.

No, Jacques simply expressed his love for her.

Christ. He actually did love her. The first woman I'd ever seen him fall in love with.

I smiled into Genie's hair, still holding his hand

before the fire. "You'll dry soon, my love. Jacques did an excellent job of setting up the house before you left this evening. We are safe here." I fell silent for a moment, listened to the wood crackle while I organized my thoughts and they rested with me. "Would you mind if we stayed here for a while before heading back to the States? I wanted to show you the estate, and then go h-home." I forced the words out, making it clear where I wanted to spend my time.

Somewhere between here and there, with an ocean in between. But home wasn't a place, a location, or a pile of ancient stone bearing a title or with a name attached to a document or bearing some official ranking.

Home was where we belonged together. It simply took us a chateau, a castle and a splash in a fountain for the three of us to find it.

Thank you for reading

L ove Barclay? Read more of Rippton U, Beau Bennett and the Kingsmen in RIPPTON ALLSTARS and PLAYING TO WIN

Teaser

Read on for an excerpt of ANGEL SHOT, the next book in Rippton Creatives.

ANGEL SHOT

HELIA

"Can you see him? Anything that looks like him?" Angelica's voice spoke in my ear like some kind of undercover operative in a spy movie.

But we weren't playing spies and heroes tonight. Nope, it was Tuesday night. Death Date Night, or Death to Dating Night. Cheap night at plenty of bars, pizzerias, and diners.

Also it was Taco Tuesday, and I was missing out.

The night I tried to become Tinderella for the tenth consecutive week in a row.

And my tenth epic fail, also consecutive.

"That's it. I'm done." I shrugged, downed my

water in a tumbler to make it look like vodka because I didn't want to be sad and alone, despite how I felt.

"Stay another five minutes," Angelica urged. "You know I live vicariously through you. Give me that."

"Uh huh. And how is that facade of life going for you right now?" I snorted into my glass, talking to myself.

I mean, how sad could I possibly look? My strike rate so far wasn't particularly hot, sizzling, or even flopping.

Six stand ups, and four half shows of the 'my mother is dying and I have to leave' hurrying off variety.

It was like no man on Rippton U's wealthy offspring inhabited campus would come within sneezing distance of me. I might as well have a sign that proclaimed 'anathema' stamped to the top of my head for all and sundry to see.

Angelica rattled on, impervious to my moods, as always. "I get to pretend to leave my apartment, sit in a cafe, and sip water, all whilst *not* infecting the local area with my hyperactivity, or my crippling anxiety. You know, whichever lands first."

"I think you get the better part of this deal," I

said dryly. "Alright. His time is up. It's been forty minutes. Enough is enough."

"Oh, girl. Go flirt with the bartender."

"It's a girl."

"So? Go get laid. A change of pace never hurt."

Yeah, but there is no pace, and no one is getting laid.

"You mean the diner server?" I eyed said waitress who winked at me, letting a quick fantasy play out in my head. A moment later my glass wasn't the only damp thing about the table.

The little diner just outside campus limits was still a favorite haunt for locals and students alike. A presence that all the wealth in the kingdom wasn't indeed theirs, and that they could live a normal life, offspring of billionaires all of them.

cough us *cough*

More fakeness and bullshit.

I bought into it just like everyone else.

"Um, yeah," Angelica replied sheepishly.

"Girl in the chair, thank you for spending another amazing Tuesday Not Date Night with yours truly."

"Talk to you next week, sister," Angelica sent air kisses and signed off.

I pulled the earpiece out, turned it over and

dropped the tiny miracle of technology into my black glitter purse, the item totally out of place in the white and red splashed retro themed milkshake bar-cum-diner that served alcohol after ten P.M.

The bell over the door tinkled. I craned my neck to watch who came in, praying it wasn't my late date now that I'd made my choice to go the hell home.

Two tired cops on their local beat, each grumpier looking than the last, entered the diner, marring the colorful facade with their gritty noir darkness which made it my cue to *really* leave.

Date Night is done for another week.

"Fuck me, my life is sad," I muttered, finishing my water.

"You want a coffee to go, sweetie?" The waitress appeared at my table on cue.

"Thanks, Misha. Appreciate you." I made a heart with my hands and she ruffled my hair.

"I won't be a minute, date girl."

She didn't lie; in less than sixty seconds I clutched a tall, black, burned coffee that singed my insides and clung to them like so much ash as I made the diner door tinkle on my way out, waving to my regular waitress.

"Sooo sad," I sang to the night air, scaring a sleeping quail that hightailed it along the dimly lit path I took, darting side to side in a flurry like a suicide chicken as it assumed I chose to chase it.

Run, run, birdie.

I giggled at the tiny creature's antics as it veered off the path and disappeared beneath a bush. A pair of luminous, disembodied eyes peered back at me.

"Night night, cutie."

I blew the quivering quail a kiss, and turned off at the next fork away from campus and the lecture halls at the exclusive, rich kid and legacy alumni admissions only college.

Rippton wasn't a place where I thought I'd spend my newly found freedom, but my parents paid the tithes to be rid of the only child they never seemed to want, seeing as I didn't fit into their *perfect progeny* mould while I inherited a boatload of abandonment issues and an apartment of my choice on the edge of town.

Sororities and parties never did it for me. Perching on my window seat, a glass of red wine dangling from my hand as I watched the college town grow silent each night, leaving me with the taste of dew on the icy night air, though? That did.

The same air that drifted through the arched floor to ceiling window I left open every night that was big enough for an adult to easily step through if they were willing to risk their existence over a sheer, four-story drop to the filthy streetscape below.

The nights I left my window open were the nights I slept best, as though the soft murmur of the sleepy town's night time comings and goings filtered through to me in my dream state like a conversation I could listen to but didn't have to engage in.

Hell, I'd even woken once from a dream to find a glowy, white angel standing at the end of my bed. Lost in a dream? Maybe. Cliche, but true. It took a few blinks for him to disappear, but my comfort level rose, and I clung to that pretence that all was right in the world, and that good girls went to heaven.

Not that I'd ever been the epitome of one of those, but I could pretend on that basis too.

Anyone else might freak out, but my weird happy zone appeared to be the reverse of everyone else's.

Everyone, except maybe Angelica.

The blonde anxiety bomb of a hermit rarely ventured from her apartment. Everything was ordered in, including her online classes. Thanks to her family's—wealthy—intervention, she got to study as she liked, providing she kept her marks up. Angelica was no party girl risk, and her grades never fell below a high distinction level, leaving her exactly where she wanted to be—alone.

I sipped my scalding, ashy coffee, twisted my way through the streets, and took as many different options as possible.

Angelica, your paranoia is infectious.

Just as her laughter and cheeky sense of humor that no one ever saw was contagious. It was sad, really. She was such a beautiful person, and kept it all to herself. But, preferences, and I was glad I had one commiserator in this weird little existence until I was freed from both Rippton and my family's ever-present expectations.

I laughed to myself, snuggling the warmth of my tall take away cup to my chest. The streets behind the rows of shops were silent, save for the light drizzle of rain that stopped and started on a whim. Townhouses and narrow residential alleyways turned into gritty lanes filled with rubbish of mechanics shops and commercial properties.

Somewhere behind me, tin banged on tin, the sound reverberating along the narrow light industrial street.

I quickened my steps, pushing my pace ever faster until I came to a corner, and picked the path back to suburbia. Which would have been a solid strategy on any other night, barring not-date-night, anti-Taco Tuesday.

Tonight, my choices led me straight into the arms of devils.

I barreled around the next corner, head down, hell bent on getting home to my apartment out of the rain, sending Angelica a message stating how she'd skewed my sense of everything when I slammed head first into a solid something that unfortunately for both of us wore my burnt coffee.

"Damn, I was enjoying that." I looked up, my apology on my lips. "I'm sorry. I wasn't–"

I kept looking up. And up, and up.

Right into the face of an angel.

If angels were monstrous creatures born of pale skin, white hair so fine the moonlight left traces of celestial dust on each strand, and palest blue eyes highlighted with a sliver of demonic red.

This one stood at least six and a half feet tall, with broad shoulders, and felt like steel to run face first into.

He also wore my coffee.

"I'm so sorry," I whispered, reaching out to—pat him dry, try to wipe the mess away—but his expression stopped me.

Disgust.

"Oh. Um, I hope that comes out. I'll just be—"

A second angel appeared slightly behind the first, as close to identical as my artist's eye could tell in the dark night, despite the starlight tracing their sharp features made for demons and put in the wrong body.

I twisted back, *knowing* my instinct served me wrong, only inciting the predators lurking within those beautiful bodies, and stopped, already face to nipple height with the next. The first turned on his heel in a delicate as fuck pivot better suited to a dance floor than an alley I should never have set foot in, sandwiching me between their bodies, effectively blocking my path.

I bit my lip, edging sideways. They came too, reducing my exit options to exactly zilch.

The second angel raised his hand, stroking a slicked finger across my cheek. "She's so much prettier when she's awake. I thought it was the other way around."

"Much prettier," the first agreed. "Especially with the addition of blood." A cool hand caught my chin, tilting my head back from behind me so the angel-demon there could stare into my upside down eyes.

I blinked, recognizing the features I tried so hard

to wash away with my wakefulness as the truth I tried so hard to ignore and deny in my waking hours slammed into me.

"I painted you. My angel," I blurted. "My seraph." That last came out on a whisper. A breath.

A confession.

READ ANGEL SHOT

ABOUT THE AUTHOR

USA Today Bestselling author Sofia Aves writes fast-paced police romances, sizzling military units, steamy cowboys with a Montana backdrop and the occasional cheeky god. Sofia writes kidlit for charity and has over one hundred and fifty publications across five not-so-super-secret pen names. As acquisitions editor for Evernight and Evernight Teen publishing she loves discovering new talent in romance and YA spaces, and is a mum of three crazies in a returned veteran household. Sofia has two overly large fur babies who think they're teacup puppies, a duck who prefers to eat from a dog bowl and two axolotls named after a dragon and a firebird.

Sofia lives near Brisbane, Australia where she has her own alpaca park, Lorendel.

www.sofiaaves.com

Sign up to **Sofia's newsletter** and get a free Blue Blooded Brothers book.

Haven't read the Z Boy's prequel? Get it for free here:
A TABLE FOR TEN
Follow Sofia on
BookBub
Twitter
Instagram

READ SOFIA'S SERIES

Blue Blooded Brothers
    Collision
    Politics & Paperwork
Blindsided
Sentinel
Mugshots & Candy Canes
Impact
Reckoning
Red Hart Ranch
Snow on the Range
Siren on the Range
Sundown on the Range
Spirit on the Range
Ash on the Range (2025)

Mistletoe on the Range (2025)

Forgotten Mountain Man

Texan Devils

Ranger's Wish

Ranger Bedevilled

Ranger's Passion

Ranger's Fury

Ranger's Wrath

Ranger's Storm

Snapdragons & Seductions

Summer with a Ranger

Merry with a Ranger

Playing to Win

Off Boarding

Vicious Slash

Zero Pointer

Off Stage Fling

Rippton Allstars

Crushing It

Glacial Force

Rippton Creatives

Study Games

Make Me, Break Me

Twisted Obsession

Spring Break with a Mafia Prince

A Royally Fake French Menage

Jericho Chimeras

Puck Me Always

Puck My Heart

Puck me Sideways

Z Boys

King

Joker

Hearts

Ace

Mayhem & Mistletoe

Ruski

Fast Track to Love

Speed Trap

Klauss Brothers

Zander

Keegan

Gallo Empire *with Jade Marshall*

Splintered Vows

Fractured Vows

Fierce Vows

Savage Covenant

Rom Coms

She's A Hot Christmas Mess

Boats, Moats and Root Beer Floats

Writing Romantasy as

SOFIA SHELLEY

Dead Poets Sorority

Writing Reverse Harem Dark Romance as

DOVE PRIEST

Recurve Ridge

Kidlit writing as

JO SEYSENER

The OCD Elf

The OCD Elf's Great Reindeer Calamity

Greg and the Egg

writing YA as

JOSS PHOENIX

Alchem Academy

Writing spicy paranormal romance as

RAVEN HUSH

Club Fray

Darkest Desires

Purge

Kidnapped By Claws

Ruin

Shadow Lords

Sinner's End

Heaven's Gate (2026)

Monster Brides

Phoenix's Eternal Flame

Kraken's Vow

Krampus' Christmas Bride

Silent Sentinels Duet

Reflections of Silence

Echoes in the Void

Monsters In New York

Feral Moon Rising (2025)

www.ingramcontent.com/pod-product-compliance
Lightning Source LLC
Chambersburg PA
CBHW050837180626
46814CB00007B/2506